BESTSELLER

Books by Christopher Knight

St. Helena
Ferocity
The Laurentian Channel
Bestseller

BESTSELLER

a novel by

CHRISTOPHER
KNIGHT

AudioCraft Publishing, Inc.

This book contains the complete
unabridged text of the original work.

BESTSELLER

An AudioCraft Publishing, Inc. book
published by arrangement with the author

Cover layout by Chuck Beard - Straits Area Printing

For information, address:
AudioCraft Publishing, Inc.
PO Box 281
Topinabee Island, MI. 49791

ISBN: 1-893699-20-X

AudioCraft Books are published by
AudioCraft Publishing, Inc., PO Box 281, Topinabee Island, MI 49791

Printed in the United States of America

First Printing - June, 2002

This book was filmed entirely on location in Michigan

Written and Directed by Christopher Knight

Editing and Technical assistance provided by
Deirdre Knight

Casting by: Mind's Eye

Cinematography by Cindee Rocheleau, Sheri Kelley,
Jevona Livingston, Diane Gurnee

Graphics and special effects by Chuck Beard
and
Straits Area Printing

Catering and lodging provided by
The Camel Riders Restaurant & Resort, Wetmore, Michigan

Musical entertainment provided by:
Tony Iommi
Type-O Negative
Blue Oyster Cult

Author's Note

On a particular night in May, 2001, I was awakened from a sound sleep. I hadn't been dreaming, or, if I had, I certainly had no recollection. Nothing unusual for me, or anyone else for that matter.

Regardless, on this particular night, I was unable to return to sleep. I booted up my HP laptop and went to work on the outline for an idea I'd recently had. Nothing new. I get a dozen ideas a day, and every week or two, one interests me enough to sketch it into a basic outline. I have a bunch of these now; few will probably ever make it past that simple stage.

But this idea was, I felt, unique.

The story would be set in an area familiar to me (as most of my writings are) but would involve certain aspects of the business that I am currently employed. The synopsis, the outline of the book, was completed in under four hours on that particular night.

However, throughout the summer, I became bogged down with other projects (most notably a well-received series of children's books that I've penned under the pseudonym *Johnathan Rand*).

This particular story kept drifting back into my mind like my wife's cooking. (No, it's not shameless brown-nosing: she really is a fabulous chef.)

Realizing that the book would never be written without some diligent discipline, I traveled to the area where I believed my story would take place: a remote cabin on a tiny lake, in a rather secluded area in Michigan's upper peninsula. Alone, at the end of August. I gave myself seven days. I would, I told myself, write *Bestseller* in exactly one week. Not including rewrites, of course. But the basic first draft, the entire *story,* would be complete.

The area in which I hid became the backdrop, the stage for *Bestseller.* I awoke around two a.m. every morning and wrote until dawn, when I would pick up my fishing rod and slink down to the dock to throw a few unsuccessful casts into the water. Twenty minutes later, I'd be in front of my laptop again. (I do everything on a laptop these days, just for the sheer convenience. Plus, if I ever get *really* pissed off at it, I can sling it right out the window quite easily.)

On the very first morning, I rowed across the small lake and caught site of a meager cabin that sat alone, tucked beneath thick trees. I snapped a photo with one of those six-dollar disposable cameras I bought at the Cheboygan K-Mart, and the result is what you see on the cover of this book. Presto. The cabin that I saw that morning became Anne Harper's cabin. You'll be meeting her in a moment.

That week was some of the most furious, most intense writing I have ever done. I began on a Tuesday, and ended the following Tuesday. The last day of writing was a blur, a marathon session from midnight Monday until exactly nine p.m. on Tuesday. Twenty-one hours, pausing only to nuke a can of *Power Ranger Spaghetti-O's*, the writer's staple.

When I write, certain songs become a subliminal canvas for me. I often write with music blaring, other times in stony silence. For *Bestseller,* Tony Iommi's solo CD (simply entitled *Iommi)* became, in a very literal sense, the soundtrack of the story. Or vice-versa; I'm not sure which. The ominous, dark chords just seemed to mesh with the theme and pace of the book. I've admired Tony's work for years as a founder of the heavy metal band *Black Sabbath.* If you want to hear guitar work that will leave blisters on your skin, pick up a copy of *Iommi.*

My thanks to the Camel Rider's Resort and Restaurant in Wetmore, Michigan, for their kind hospitality. See you again.

And one more note:

Although it has been stated on the legal page of this book that it is a work of fiction, I find the need to stress that the characters and incidents are completely fictitious. I still have people who come up to me and say things like *'hey, that character in that one book . . . you were writing about so-and-so, weren'tcha?'* No. I wasn't, and I haven't. Or, as Gerald Morgan puts it to Anne Harper, *'it's only a story, Ms. Harper . . . .'*

I hope you enjoy.

Christopher Knight
May, 2002

As the needle
Finds the vein;
As the bullet goes
Through the brain;
As you're swimming
Into sea;
As you're drowning
Think of me—
The laughing man in the devil mask . . . .

—Tony Iommi; *The Laughing Man in the Devil Mask*

BESTSELLER

one

It might have been the way the tall pines shuddered in the gentle, morning breeze. Or the delicate, slow-motion ripples on the small lake in the early sunshine. Or the shiny-green hummingbirds as they buzzed hurriedly from flower to feeder, feeder to flower, then zipped off into the misty forest. It might have been the wind slipping through the maple trees and the way each leaf moved, like tiny green hands waving to the crowd along a parade route. It might have been a thousand more things, a million things—

But it wasn't.

It was just the simple beauty of nature that caused Anne Harper to pause before opening the car door. She gazed, awestruck, through the bug-streaked windshield. Heaved a satisfied sigh. She turned the key and the churning engine stopped instantly. The air conditioner hissed tiredly, heaved a final, sputtering breath, and died. Anne placed her hands on the wheel, drew a breath, and just—

Watched.

It's like yesterday. Like I never left at all.

When she finally *did* open the car door and step outside, her senses were washed with still more delights from the cool morning. The scents of punky cedar and gummy pine, of damp moss and dew-filled grass. A dozen varieties of wildflowers grew on the southern side of a small cabin, and their delicate fragrances haunted the morning breeze. The morning had a pure, evangelistic quality, and Anne was instantly born-again. Keep the fire and brimstone to yourself, thank you very much, hallelujah, amen, and all that.

She closed the car door, breathed in deeply, stretched, yawned. Exhaled slowly.

Gazed.

Unpacking could wait. Feeling tired could wait. *Everything* could wait.

At least a few more minutes, anyway.

She'd driven all night—twelve hours—from New York City to Michigan's upper peninsula. Six hundred miles and two complete, unabridged audio books. *Pop Goes the Weasel,* by James Patterson. *Black Notice,* by Patricia Cornwell. Time flew.

And beyond the car: a million streetlights and a billion shimmering stars. The city had slipped away quickly and quietly. Rural America, all sleepy and silent and dark, passed by in village signs, sparse homes, small towns. Over numerous bridges and culverts, through inky fields and still forests. Two tanks of gas, a half-dozen coffees, and the frequent restroom stops that they prompted. The drive had been a long one, for sure, but she hadn't wanted to stop. Certainly not for the night, anyway. She would bear with the long journey, the winding roads, the tired eyes. Arrive at the cabin mid-morning. Then she would take a short walk down to the dock, and then . . . .

As she walked, the sun came up behind her, its warm hands caressing her back. Insects buzzed. Nearby, a kingfisher slipped noiselessly from the top of a limbless, dead tree that rose up from the water's edge. The bird swooped low and glided mere inches over the glossy surface until it arced back up to perch on yet another tree, continuing its morning hunt for food. Below, beneath the surface, small fish darted in the shallows around the dock, warily suspicious of the shadowy figure that made its way along the graying planks.

And the city died. The honks and the sirens, the breaking glass and tire squeals were gone. The subway clatter and murmuring traffic vanished. She could actually *feel* the city seeping from the pores of her skin, swirling down some unseen drain, until the sights and sounds of New York were drowned out by the deafening roar of pure, pristine —

Silence.

She stopped at the end of the dock, placed her hands in

the back pockets of her jeans, and watched. The surface of the lake was like chrome, and the trees mirrored on the clear water. The sky was a rich, virgin blue, cloudless.

And Anne felt *good.* Her soul lightened and took flight. Softly, gently, soaring up, higher and higher, weightless, until she felt like her whole body would lift from the dock, drifting up over the trees, across the lake, into the sky. She raised her arms like wings, child-like, as if it were possible, as if she really *could* fly. Closed her eyes. Exhaled. Smiled.

Silly, she thought. *But it feels good. I'm glad I'm here, even with what's going on. I'm glad I'm—*

two

—*alone.*

That's what you're thinking, Anne. I know it. I know you.

The stalker watched from a distance, well-hidden within twisted, congested brush. He had watched the silver BMW roll to a stop in the dirt driveway. Watched her yawn, stretch, walk across the grass to the dock.

You think you're alone, but you're not. Not at all.

Insects swirled about his concealed face, mosquitos and tiny black flies, but he didn't take notice.

Yes. This is perfect. Better than perfect.

He watched her as she took in the day, watched her admire her surroundings. She was lost in the moment, trapped in time, and he felt as though he could emerge from the forest and she probably wouldn't notice him . . . or even care if she did.

And he felt *powerful.* He felt almighty and omnipotent, god-like. Of course, this was nothing new. He'd felt like this before, on numerous occasions. It was the feeling that he lived for, the feeling of being in total control of another's destiny. Holding the cards for someone else, playing their hand when *he* felt it was time.

And each time it was better, more powerful than the last.

And what's this? Are you going to fly, Annie? Flap your wings and take off? Go ahead and try.

He smiled, and slowly swept a mosquito from his eyebrow. It had been biting him for some time, and now he crushed it against his brow with his forefinger. The tiny insect balled up as he swept it away, leaving a thin trail of blood on his skin.

Try to fly, Anne. Even if you could, it wouldn't help you. Not anymore. You're mine now, Anne Harper. Ladies and gentlemen, boys and girls. Grandmas and grandpas, aunts and uncles. Take your seats, folks. Take your seats . . . the show is about to begin.

three

Anne turned around and looked at her home for the next week: a small cabin that sat only a few feet from the water's edge. It was an old structure, but not unkempt, and certainly not unattended. A stone foundation supported evenly constructed, weathered pine logs, the color of honey and summer. A newly-reshingled roof glowed forest-green in the sun. One large window, in front of the small dining room, faced the lake. It was flanked by two other smaller windows, one on either side. In front of the dining room window a hummingbird feeder dangled from a cedar limb, and two of the tiny birds were partaking in the sweet sugar water.

"You outdo yourself every year, George." Anne whispered the

words and smiled, shaking her head slowly. George Otto owned the cabin and rented it out during the summer months for a steep, yet well-deserved premium. He was a flawless caretaker, and, except for the new roof and a few more bird feeders, Anne swore that the cabin hadn't changed by one dust speck since the first time she saw it.

She'd been coming to the cabin for two weeks, every summer, for the past ten years. Or was it eleven? She'd forgotten herself. Years ago, the retreat had been suggested by another literary agent when Anne had confessed that she was having a difficult time concentrating on new manuscripts. *Can't pick manuscripts if you don't have the time to read them,* she'd said. *No manuscripts, no writers. No writers, no book sales to publishers. No sales, no commissions. No commissions . . . no job.*

So, through a friend of a friend who had a brother who knew someone who had an uncle who knew someone else, she'd found this place. A small, one-bedroom cabin—stolen from the pen of Terry Redlin or Thomas Kincaid, no doubt— nestled beneath the pines and cedars and birches that surrounded Lost Lake. The name of the lake fit, too, as one would have to travel nearly seven miles of dirt roads before traversing another four miles over a rough, uneven two-track to reach the water's edge.

The nearest village, Three Corners, population seventy-three, was twenty miles away. It was gloriously modest as small towns go. Norman Rockwell could have sued. Gas station. Post office. One market. One church and three bars, which probably meant something; whatever *that* was, no one could really say. And not a single stop light in Three Corners. Not even a flashing yellow caution light, and Jesus . . . every village has one of those.

Years ago, on her first trip to the cottage, Anne's car bumped and knocked across the rugged two-track. She swore there was nothing on earth that could be worth this much trouble.

She was wrong.

The cabin became her yearly getaway, her hideout from the world. Here, she rested, she read, she worked. Her head cleared, her mind focused, her soul re-energized. There was no phone, no fax, no e-mail or internet. No CNN or FOX or ABC or CBS or NBC. Not even regular rural mail delivery. Communication was an old *Cobra* citizen's band radio that sat on the mantle of the cabin's fieldstone fireplace. The black-and-tan battery-operated unit was an early model, the kind you might see at a yard sale or flea market with a note that said *'works good—$1.00'*. The tiny coiled cobra insignia was faded and chipped. The radio only transmitted and received two channels; channel 14, which was a common channel used by truckers on the highway twenty miles away (as well as a few other hermits without phone service); and channel 9, the emergency channel monitored by the sheriff's department. George Otto had shown her how to use the radio years ago; Anne hadn't turned it on since. Television, faxes, e-mails, hell, smoke signals for that matter . . . she came here to get away from all that. For two weeks here, every summer. How was it that one of her friends had put it?

Oh, yes.

Incommunicado. Not available for communication. On your own, baby, on your own.

Well, not *last* summer. Last summer, the trip had been canceled. But that couldn't be helped. Last summer was all a blur, anyway. A nightmare, really. Of doctors and needles and medication and sterile rooms and worrying and waiting and wondering. Trips to Mayo clinic in Minnesota. Strange hotels and midnight flights back to New York. More tests, more drugs, more prodding needles.

And tears. *Lots* of tears. *Oceans* of tears.

But that was behind her. *Them.*

Hopefully.

Two years ago, when she'd discovered a lump in her left breast, her own mortality came screaming at her from out of nowhere, as it always does when your own future is in question.

Cancer? Me? There's a mistake. I'm too young. Too healthy. I'm too—

Human.

She was thirty-three then, and the lump had been removed successfully. They'd caught it early enough. It was a scare, but she'd won *that* one.

Her doctor had described cancer as an animal, a beast that seems to show up without warning, without regards to anything or anyone. Cancer didn't care if you were healthy, didn't care if you were a runner, or whether or not you ate your bran flakes every morning or whether or not you ate your veggies. Cancer was indiscriminate; all it cared about was itself. Feeding itself to survive, to stay alive. A home-grown terrorist.

And Anne had been lucky.

She'd found the lump while showering. It hadn't been the first time that she'd noticed a small, marble-sized knot. The first time had been in college; the lumps turned out to be benign and had been attributed to drinking too much caffeine. When she ditched the coffee, the lumps went away. Simple as that. Ever since, she'd been careful about her coffee drinking. Tea became her beverage of choice, except, of course, last night. Plenty of Starbucks last night, that's for sure. A one night coffee binge wasn't going to hurt.

So when she'd discovered another lump only a couple of years ago, she hadn't been overly worried. Puzzled, yes.

Caffeine? I haven't had hardly any since . . .

And then, of course, a pathologic evaluation, and the biopsy results. The phone call from the doctor's office.

Hello? Mrs. Harper? Yes, Doctor Scheare would like to see you today.

The following weeks had been a blur.

Cancer? What do you mean, cancer? Me? Anne Harper? Hell, I'm only . . . .

There had been surgery to remove the small cyst, followed by hormonal therapy. Tamoxifen. The drug made her nauseous, but, compared to the alternative, she could live with the side effects.

So, when Anne's seven year-old daughter was diagnosed with leukemia in January of last year, her own battle with cancer seemed ridiculous. Ludicrous, actually. In the face of what the monster would do to her daughter, her own fight with the disease seemed trivial. It wasn't, of course. No battle with cancer is ever trivial. But that's what it seemed like to Anne.

Please, no. Not my baby. Not little Allie.

Eight months later, the miracle of miracles. Allison had pulled through. It hadn't been easy, from the initial diagnosis, the hospitals, the endless drugs, and the chemotherapy that held her on the brink of death for a week. Anne had been told on August 10th at two forty-six in the morning (she'd never forget the day or the time) to prepare for the worst. Allison wouldn't make it through the night. They had done all they could.

Sometimes the monster comes out of nowhere, Anne, Allie's doctor had told her. *There are no reasons. He just shows up. There's nothing you could have done differently.*

On December 10th, 2000, Allison Rose Harper celebrated her eighth birthday—exactly four months after she'd been written off by the best specialists in the country. On December 24th, Christmas Eve, a phone call from Dr. Gardner, Allie's doctor at Mayo. He was dumbfounded.

Are you ready for this?

No.

Take a breath.

Okay.

It's gone. Completely. Merry Christmas, Anne. Merry Christmas. Allie beat the beast. She's cancer-free, Anne. This is me talking. She won. We won.

There would be more tests, of course. There would always be more tests, sometimes once a month. Routine.

But now—

Now, there was *another* phone call. A few weeks ago, from Dr. Gardner.

I've found something I'd like to look at, Anne. It's probably nothing, but I want to run some expanded tests on Allison . . . .

More tests.

No. Stop it, Anne. Stop thinking about it. She took a deep breath, let it out. Took another. Here the air was so fresh, so clean, so . . . unlike the city.

Far out on the lake, two mallard ducks, male and female, winged in. They skidded to a splashing halt on the glossy surface.

She's going to be fine. They're just tests. Probably nothing.

After Dr. Gardner's call, she had abruptly canceled her plans to return to the cottage on Lost Lake. *How can I leave now?* she thought. It was a decision that had been countered by nearly everyone. Her staff, her friends, even Allie's doctor. *You need this, Annie,* they all told her. The test results wouldn't be back for weeks, and Allison will be fine. *Is* fine. *Leave Allison with Marta. Go. You need to rest. Go read some manuscripts. Writers are your livelihood, Anne. You can't negotiate book deals with publishers if you have nothing to offer them. And besides . . . there are some great writers waiting for you to discover them. Take your two weeks.*

One. I'll take one week.

Fine. Book it. No pun intended, honest. Book your week.

Leaving Allie with Marta, her long-time housekeeper-nanny, had been hard. This was the year that she'd promised her daughter that she could come with her to northern Michigan. *We'll go for walks, we'll toast marshmallows over a fire. We'll swim. And we'll fish, Allie. There are lots of fish in the lake.* The latter prospect delighted the child, and she had been looking forward to the new adventure all summer.

More tests. We need more tests. You go, Anne, but leave Allie here. With Marta. Just in case.

With wisdom well beyond her eight years, Allie said she understood.

But you're not going to go fishing without me, are you, mommy? Break-your-heart tears in her eyes. *Are you?*

Absolutely not.

Promise? Cross your heart?

Promise. Cross my heart.

four

Ten a.m. Unpacking. The routine was deja vu. Same things she'd always brought with her. Shirts go here, just like they always did, in the same cedar dresser she'd always placed them. Underwear and socks here, in the drawer that stuck if you pulled it open too far. Closet items over here. Paper towels go in the dispenser, bath towels in the bathroom. What groceries she'd brought she placed in the cupboards. There were a few perishable items that she'd need, items that wouldn't have kept during the trip. She'd pick them up tomorrow evening when she traveled to Three Corners.

And Allie-Gator. The beanie baby.

She'd bought the critter in Minnesota last year, in the 'dark days' of Allie's illness. It was goofy-looking, with overemphasized teeth and large, bulging eyeballs. The green creature was placed at Allison's bedside where it stood watch over the fragile child during her chemo. Allison had taken an immediate and affectionate liking to the stuffed animal, hence its name: *Allie-Gator.* Since Allison couldn't go on this trip with her, she'd insisted that Allie-Gator join her mother for the week, to watch over her and keep her safe.

Anne picked up the creature and placed it on the nightstand, then returned to the small dining room and sat down at the table.

The cabin had been furnished in mostly Rittenhouse furniture. The old stuff. The *good* stuff. It was sturdy and solid, and the wood had faded gracefully with age. The cushions on the couch had been replaced several years ago, but they were the only additions that she could spot. Everything else looked the same. Same tongue-in-groove knotty pine on the walls, dulled to a very seventies orange-yellow. Same hand-hewn cedar beams supporting the roof, same smooth-as-glass hardwood floor. Same green and brown throw rug in front of the fireplace, with the same quarter-sized burn spot in the upper right corner. Same everything. Perfect.

She stretched and yawned, finally allowing herself to be tired from the all-night drive. Two skyscrapers of manilla envelopes—various manuscripts—were piled on the floor near the couch. They would wait. Her eyes were heavy, her body drained. She stood up and walked to the bedroom, petted the green monster next to her bed. "Keep good watch, Allie-Gator," she yawned.

Sleep came easy.

It was nearing one in the afternoon when she awoke. The day had warmed and the cabin was stuffy. Anne opened up the remaining windows, allowing the breeze to sift throughout the cottage.

And the door. She opened the heavy oak door and fresh air drifted through the screen. She was about to walk away, then—

On the porch was a nine-inch by twelve-inch beige envelope. Thick, too. Full. It looked like any of the dozens of packages her office received each week. Like any of the numerous manuscripts she had brought to the cabin to review.

Yet—

How did it get here? She hadn't dropped it while unpacking. You don't just drop a two-pound package and not know it.

She scanned the woods. Sun glossed the thick, green foliage, and birds flitted through the trees. Here, there was no mail delivery. And there was only one other cabin, on the far side of the lake. Anne had never met the owner, whom George had told her was a retired man in his fifties. He'd told her his name, a Steven something-or-another; Anne couldn't remember. A trail wound around the lake to the home, but she'd never ventured to the other cottage on the other side of the lake.

She pushed open the screen, stepped outside, and picked up the envelope, once again scanning the forest as if she might see a blue-suited *Federal Express* courier or a brown-cloaked *UPS* driver slipping off into the woods. She saw no one.

She turned the envelope over. It was hand-addressed to her, to her New York office. No return address, though. No postmark. She must have brought this one with her, after all.

No. Wait. I couldn't have.

When she chose the manuscripts to bring with her, she had scribbled the name of the author on the outside of the envelope with a fat *Sharpie* pen. The envelope in her hands did not bear her writing.

Rural courier, she thought. *Of course.* Several years ago, she'd needed some materials from her office. Some *Wite-Out,* a few highlighter pens, some stationery and several yellow legal pads. A box had been shipped to the village twenty miles away, and a courier had traveled the dirt roads to make the delivery to the tune of seventy-five dollars, not including tip.

But if it was a courier, why didn't they knock? All this way and no tip?

Puzzled, she stepped back inside the cabin, still staring at the package in her hands.

How did this get here? And—

The screen door banged closed behind her, and she sat down at the table. She sliced open the envelope with a fingernail, withdrew the contents, and glanced at the cover letter. She recognized the name instantly, and she recoiled.

Oh shit. Jesus. Not him. Not again.

five

"Gerald Morgan?"

She frowned as she whispered the name, then turned and looked back at the porch where she'd discovered the manuscript.

But how did he know I was here? How did he—

Gerald Morgan had been sending her manuscripts for years. Bad ones. *Horrible* ones. His submissions rambled for pages and pages with no clear plots or motives. Titles like *Dark Day in Hell,* and *Give the Devil His Due.* He'd never even so much as sent her a query letter to see if she might be interested in seeing his work. And God—the *presentation.* Often, she'd receive a manuscript from Morgan with no cover letter, no introduction whatsoever. Just a stack of white paper with the title printed in bold-face on the front. All of his work was typed on what must have been an ancient Royal typewriter. A *manual* typewriter. Which wasn't *too* out-of-the-ordinary. Anne had several authors under contract that used a manual typewriter, even in this day of personal computers and word processors. She even had a few clients that wrote out their novels longhand.

But Morgan's pages were littered with hastily scratched corrections (if he'd caught any mistakes, or even bothered to look for them) and coffee stains. Chapters might be out of order, or pages might be missing. In addition, the typewriter showed its age through splotchy, splattered letters that were often difficult to read. Two years ago, Anne had sent Morgan a letter, asking that he please not submit any more of his work to her. The letter had been professional, but firm.

Morgan became enraged. He called her office, and when she refused to speak with him, he went off like a pipe bomb, screaming at Candace, Anne's secretary. She hung up on him.

Two hours later he had arrived, unannounced, at the office. How he had made it through security to the 34th floor of a high rise in New York was a mystery. He had lashed out at Candace once again, hurling racial slurs and expletives like jagged knives. It was the first Anne had seen of him in person, and she was repulsed by his matted, unkempt hair and his scraggly, Grizzly Adams beard. His shirt was filthy and he reeked of heavy cigarette smoke. His eyes bulged like he had purposely pumped them full of air just for the effect, ping-pong balls with pupils.

Security had finally removed him, but not before he had smashed a glass coffee table and overturned several chairs. Later, Anne had read that he had finally been hospitalized for an undisclosed mental illness after threatening a tenant with a knife in his apartment building.

She leafed through his manuscript. Still type-written, but it seemed to be much more error-free than his previous work. Unless he didn't bother to make any corrections, which was entirely possible with Gerald Morgan.

And a *cover letter,* for gosh sakes. There was an actual cover letter, written to her. That was a first. She picked it up and read it.

Dear Ms. Harper:

First, I wish to apologize for my past behavior. It's a long story that I will not bore you with. Just please understand that, due to a malady beyond my control, I have 'not been myself' as the saying goes. I am much better, and I wish to express that I am very sorry for any undue stress I have caused you.

She stopped at this point, and re-read the first paragraph of his letter. *Could this really be Morgan?* she thought. *Complete sentences and everything? A normal thought process? God, he sounds . . . sincere.* She continued reading.

I have submitted to you a work that I hope you will consider worthy of your representation. I

know that in the past, my writing has probably seemed a bit tedious—

Anne smiled. "Try *awful,* Mr. Morgan," she said.

—but again, I believe that this was caused by my medical condition. I'd like to ask you for one more chance. I'm not asking for a promise, just a chance. I'd like you to look over my latest work, as I do feel that it is my best yet. Far better than what I have previously submitted. I really think that this book will appeal to you. It is in the genre that particularly interests you (psychological thriller) with some intriguing twists. Moreover, it deals with an industry that you are very familiar with, and, if I dare say, you, Ms. Harper, indirectly inspired the storyline. I think you'll—

Her interest was piqued, and she read faster.

—find that the story is fast-paced, well-plotted, and well-written . . . exactly what a psychological thriller should be. The story is about a beautiful literary agent who, while vacationing at a small, remote cabin, is stalked by a deranged killer. The book is called 'BESTSELLER'. A short synopsis is on the following page.

Anne stopped reading. Her heart jack-hammered in her chest, and she felt hot. She glanced nervously around, peering out the cottage windows, her eyes searching the lush, wooded surroundings.

"Holy shit," she breathed. Then again. *"Holy shit."*

She returned her gaze to the cover letter, then flipped it over to read the synopsis.

six

BESTSELLER, BY GERALD MORGAN.

Anne scanned the page quickly, her eyes darting from one paragraph to the next, then back again. Her heart pounded heavier. If he was doing this to get her attention, he'd done it. She continued reading.

'Bestseller' is the story of a New York literary agent named Beth Huston. Huston is divorced with one child. Every summer, she travels to a remote cabin on a lake. This is her sabbatical, her time away to review manuscripts and gather new clients. There are no other houses around, and the closest town is miles away.

Anne's mind spun.

However, there is one writer who she has repeatedly rejected. This writer so very much wishes to be published, yet he is constantly ignored and rejected by the agent. As his hatred for this agent and the publishing industry grows, he decides that if she will not represent him or his work, he will make it so that she won't represent anyone. And he has the perfect opportunity . . . for he knows where she goes for her retreat. He knows the land, he's been studying it. He knows that no one else is around.

Anne's skin felt hot. Her face flushed. She stopped reading and glanced nervously out the windows. A hummingbird sat at the feeder that hung from the branch just beyond the dining room window. The lake was a glimmering sheet of beveled glass, marred only by a soft breeze that smudged the shiny surface. On the other side of the lake, she stared at the only other cabin. A single crow winged over the trees, chased by several screeching blue jays. She returned her gaze to the cover letter in her hand.

Sound familiar, Ms. Harper? I hope so! I've used your setting and scenario as the basis for BESTSELLER. I hope you enjoy it.

And again, I wish to apologize for my past behavior. I offer no excuses, but, should we have the opportunity to meet face to face again (and I hope we do!) I'll explain further, and give you some insight as to why I acted the way I did. Should you,

however, decide that 'BESTSELLER' isn't quite what you're looking for, I will respectfully thank you for your valuable time.

Enjoy yourself, and I look forward to hearing from you upon your return here to New York.

Her tension eased. The growing balloon of stress sprung a slow leak, and she allowed it to empty, all of it, until the balloon was deflated.

Clever, she thought, flashing an *I can't believe I fell for that* smile. She exhaled and shook her head. *Really clever.* Morgan had been able to get her attention, and she truly *was* intrigued. Maybe not intrigued enough to read his entire manuscript—she doubted that any medication could help *his* writing—but interested enough that she *might* take a short peek at *BESTSELLER.*

First things first, though. There were other, more palatable offerings to go over. She'd carefully selected the manuscripts she'd brought; they'd be first. If she had time to read any of Morgan's work, well, then she might have a look.

She pushed *Bestseller* to the side of the table, then, after a moment of thought, picked it up and placed it on the floor. She had plenty of other things that would be piled on the table. Morgan's submission would only be in the way.

The lake, shiny and silvery in the afternoon sun, called to her. She changed into a pair of khaki shorts and a fresh blouse, and walked barefoot to the water's edge.

The water was take-your-breath-away cold, as it always had been, even ankle-deep. It iced her skin and sent a shiver through her body. She clenched her fists and hunched her shoulders tight, drawing in a loud breath through clenched teeth. The lake was spring-fed, and didn't warm up like many other inland lakes did during the summer months.

Enough of that, Anne. Brr.

She stepped out of the water and walked down the dock. The weathered planks groaned, revealing their age. A few inches beneath the surface of the lake, a crayfish recoiled and backed away, threatening the giant trespasser with two over-sized claws. White snail shells peppered the sandy bottom like tiny, ghostly skulls. All around her, small, neon-blue damselflies skittered about, their fluttering wings crackling like wax paper as they buzzed past.

At the end of the dock, a bluegill no larger than a coffee saucer was carefully stalking a bug on the surface. The fish vanished when the intruder ventured too close. The bug, a small, black beetle, escaped. Anne again found herself in awe, taking in the beauty of the day. She sighed.

Oh Allie, she thought. She placed her hands on her hips. *Next year. I promise. Next year, baby.* After a few moments she walked back to shore, completely unaware that she was being watched.

seven

Everything had gone perfectly. He had watched her enter the cabin, watched her walk into the bedroom. It had been risky to get so close to the window, but he knew that she would be asleep. She'd driven all night; she'd be tired.

And he had been right, as usual. He was *always* right.

He had crept close to the open window and peered through the screen. She was on her side, facing him. He had watched her sleep, and he admired her sandy-blonde wisps of silky hair nestled against her neck and cheek. He admired her body, her breasts and buttocks, the perfect curve of her jaw, her nose.

And he *hated* her. Oh, he loved her, in his own way, of course. But he *hated* her. Hated what she did and how she did it. *How dare she?* he had thought, as he watched her motionless form on the bed. He had been so close he could hear the gentle whisper of air through her nostrils, in and out, in and out as she breathed.

You bitch. You self-righteous, goddamn bitch. Do you know what I could do to you right now, Annie? I could cut your heart out. I could yank those jeans right off you and make you scream. And you would scream, Annie. God, would you scream. You know what you are? You're a whore. That's what you are. You and everyone in the fucking business. You're all whores and sluts and cunts and pimps. Do you know that, Anne Harper? You wouldn't know a good book if it bit you in the ass. But you will. Oh, you've got a hum-dinger comin' right at ya. Not like my other ones you rejected. Which were pretty goddamn good. Of course, you wouldn't know that. But this one is a real winner. A guaranteed Bestseller, Anne Harper, just like the name says. I'll bet this one is gonna knock you dead.

He had slipped quietly away from the window and placed the manuscript in a place where she was sure to see it. The porch was perfect. She would find it the moment she opened the door, and likely think that it had fallen from her bags. If she suspected something else, well, that was fine, too.

Remember, he had told himself, *chapters can be changed and rearranged at any time. It would be more fun to follow them in the correct order, of course. If we had to jump to the end of the book . . . .*

But first, he wanted to have his fun. He wanted to toy with her and play the same games that she played with her clients. The same games the whole publishing industry played. Only now, *now* . . . he would be holding the puppet strings. He would be the master of the marionette, and she would do everything that he said. After all . . . that's the way it was written. That's why it was going to be a . . . *Bestseller.*

She had slept longer than he'd expected. His camouflage clothing made him sweat, and his skin was waxy and hot beneath the heavy fabric. But he dared not move from his hiding place in the brush. Certainly not *yet,* anyway.

From where he stood, he could see through the kitchen window, which allowed him a view of the bedroom door. He'd watched her awaken and come into the small dining room, watched her open up the windows, the door. Watched her, his elation orgasmic, as she discovered the manuscript on the porch.

When she seated herself at the table, manuscript in hand, he *did* venture from his hiding place, only to find another that would give him a better view of her as she opened the sealed envelope. He watched her through compact binoculars as she read the cover letter. When she turned to look out the windows, he could see the alarm on her face.

Ooh, that's good, Anne, he thought. *You're playing the part already. You were made for this part, Annie Harper. It is YOU.*

He watched her clear the table, then disappear into the bedroom. She emerged from the cottage a few minutes later in a fresh change of clothing, and again he admired her body with obsessive lust, like a teenager who had accidentally spied the girl next door undressing and couldn't pull his eyes away.

Such a shame, Annie. Such a shame. You're so beautiful, so gorgeous. You're really going to make it hard, Anne. Really. You're going to make me hard. Hard as a fucking rock.

He remained tucked within the thick brush as she strode back along the dock and into the cabin.

eight

Where to begin.

Anne picked up a stack of manuscripts and placed them on the table. She'd planned to spend the first day of her stay re-acquainting herself with her surroundings. Now, in the tranquil stillness, she wanted nothing more than to relax on the couch and read. She had placed Morgan's submission to the side, as she had no plans at all to read his work: there were other submissions she couldn't *wait* to go over. Real writers who could form complete sentences and whole thoughts—from people who didn't trash her office.

Steve Germain's would be first. She'd met him at a convention, and he had impressed her. Polite, professional. Respectful. He had written a novel called *Fade to Night*, a story about a homicide detective who searches for a serial killer . . . only to find out the killer is his son. Not necessarily an original premise, but it's not the idea that matters. It's how the story is told. It's the weaving of the fabric, the delicious crafting of the language that will tell the tale and make the sale. Great ideas are a dime a dozen; great writers are even cheaper. Flea-market, blow-out prices. But great *storytellers* . . . now *that* is where the game begins and ends. How the story is told is how the reader is sold.

Germain's story was disappointing. It started out well, but the pace stagnated. Plus, it just wasn't *believable.* If the reader didn't *believe* it, they wouldn't *read* it. The characters in his story did silly things, *stupid* things that real characters wouldn't do—unless they'd been ordered to do so by the writer, in order to set up some situation or scene. They weren't *believable.* She jotted a few notes on the manuscript, explaining to Germain what she liked, what she didn't. She'd return the work with a standard stock cover letter. If Germain chose to read her comments and benefit from them, well, that was up to him. Besides: her standard rejection letter states that *all tastes vary, and what may not be right for one agent may be very welcomed by another. Good luck in your writing.* She meant it sincerely.

Next up was Charlene Allen, a published (and rather successful) writer. However, Allen was a writer of historical romance. This was her first attempt at a suspense thriller—and it was *awful.* No . . . *worse.* Worse than awful. Anne couldn't get more than twelve pages into it to see that, no matter what happened in the following chapters, the story was doomed. Much too flowery, much too rosy, much too . . . *unbelievable.*

"I hope this isn't setting a trend for the week," she said aloud, pushing Allen's manuscript to the side after scribbling a big 'X' on the envelope.

Mark Franklin was next, and she was hopeful. Mark had been a client of hers years ago when he'd penned *Theater of the Mine.* It was literary genius, especially for a first book from an unknown, unpublished writer. The book went on to sell over two million copies. He'd achieved literal overnight success, going from virtual poverty one day to wealth and fame the next. He'd been working as a computer technician, writing on the weekends and whenever he could find the time in between his wife and three daughters. One week he was wiring components, the next week he was on national television. Appearances on *Good Morning, America* and the *Today* show. Plus, Mark was outgoing and handsome. Likeable. He didn't fit the persona of the stereotyped hermit author.

Since *Theater of the Mine,* however, Franklin's work had fizzed. No . . . *nosedived.* He tried too hard to copy his original idea, first in sequel (which was disastrous) and then by reincarnating people that had been killed in his first book. Nothing he'd written since even came close to *Theater,* and she'd never even attempted to sell any more of his works, despite the fact that his first book was top-notch and he was a recognized name. He'd virtually disappeared from the literary world and the bookstore shelves in the past few years, and Anne hadn't heard from him in a long time.

His latest work, what she held in her hands, was called *Mind Theft.* It was the story of a psychopathic doctor who could manipulate patients by implanting the thoughts of others, therefore making the thoughts their own. Far-fetched, yes, and leaning strongly toward the sci-fi genre, which wasn't something she wanted to get into.

But it was Mark Franklin, author of *Theater of the Mine. Her* author, at least at one time. She'd be crazy not to at least take a *look* at his manuscript.

Anne scanned the synopsis, then the cover page. She began reading.

She stopped at page ten and dropped Franklin's entire manuscript to the floor in despair. The weight of the paper slapped the hard oak, and a few pages slid from the top of the pile. Anne sighed, disappointed. Some people had only one good book in them; Mark Franklin was apparently one of them. She was disheartened. Mark had been a good client, and she really was hoping that he had jumped back on track. She shook her head.

Caroline Yates, I wish you were here, she thought. Yates had been one of her clients, too. One of her first, actually, and her book, *A Smile in the Dark,* had been Anne's first sale to a publisher. The book was fabulous, and sailed to the top of the list in two short weeks. Yates was a brilliant writer: young, fresh out of college with a degree in biology, of all things. Single, attractive. Anne signed her almost immediately. Yates had penned four more books over the next two years, each one highly successful, each one unique. That was her knack. Caroline didn't stick to one particular style, and her work was *breathtaking*. Her writing carved her own niche in the psychological thriller genre. Her stories were dark, and dealt with human tragedy and depravity revolving around ritualistic serial murderers and sexual sadists. It was hard to believe that the stories churned out were penned by such an attractive, innocent-looking young woman. Caroline Yates looked like she'd be more suited to write feature articles for *Woman's Day* or holiday entertaining pieces for *Cooking Light*.

And they were friends. Caroline and Anne became close, sharing more than just a client-agent relationship. They got together often, went to parties together. Anne had been just starting out as an agent; Caroline, one of her first clients, was her cheering section in a highly competitive, screw-your-neighbor business. Before Caroline's first advance came through, Anne loaned her several thousand dollars to help with a down payment on a home. Caroline had even been a bridesmaid in Anne's wedding in 1989. They were like sisters. Best friends.

When Caroline Yates wrote a book, she kept the entire story under wraps. No one knew the title, the story line, nothing. Anne was the first to see and read it, followed by the publisher. Anne would plead . . . *beg* . . . for just a few advance chapters.

"Caroline," she had said one evening, "you're driving everybody nuts. Can't you just tell me a little bit about it?"

Giggles. "No."

"Just a bit? I won't say a word."

"Nope."

"Pretty please?"

More laughter. "Nope!"

It became a standing joke for Anne to constantly ask to read what Caroline was working on. And the answer was always the same. *Nope. You'll have to wait. But when I'm ready, Anne, you'll be the first. Promise.*

After the success of her first novel, big parties were held to announce the title and display the cover art for the new Caroline Yates book. Everybody who was anybody was there, although Caroline herself tended to think the events a bit fraudulent. She attended these parties with a polite contempt, not understanding what all the fuss was about, for gosh sakes. It's only a *book*. Still, she was professional, playing the part of the glitzy author, at least until she could sneak out and take a hit off a joint with one of the servers or caterers. Her down-to-earth good-nature, coupled with a very simple, yet unforgettable attractiveness, made Caroline Yates a *person-to-be-seen-with* in the Big Apple. Which was kind of tough, as Caroline preferred gatherings that were small and intimate, where most of the attendees wore jeans and t-shirts. Nevertheless, she enjoyed her success.

But Caroline Yates' luck was about to change. She had been working on her sixth book when she was murdered.

nine

Caroline Yates was twenty-six at the time of her death.

Anne had spoken with her the night she was killed. She was finished with the book, she'd said. Just some minor revisions. Like always, Caroline kept the story, even the title, to herself until it was in the hands of her agent. She promised to send Anne the manuscript in a few days, then head off to Vail for a weekend ski trip. She'd met some guy, she explained to Anne, that, in her words, was a cross between Michael Douglas and Mel Gibson. Caroline was as giddy about him as a seventeen-year old. And yes, she'd bragged to Anne, she *did* intend to get laid this weekend, *thank you very much.*

Her bizarre death was all over the news the following morning. Caroline Yates's body had been found outside her home in Bay Shore, on Long Island. She'd been stabbed repeatedly and left to die. After stealing any valuables she'd had, the killer set fire to the home, then fled in Caroline's Range Rover. Caroline had managed to cling to life long enough to drag herself out into the yard before the house was totally engulfed in flames. It was there that firemen found her, dead, a river of blood stretching back across the lawn, over the porch and into her home, which was now completely ablaze.

Anne Harper, and many others, had been shocked into a stupor. Caroline Yates had been well-liked by so many people. At the time of her death she had reached superstar status in the literary world, a household name and familiar face. Rows of Caroline Yates books stocked the shelves of B. Dalton, Borders, Barnes & Noble, Waldenbooks. She'd even made the cover of *People.* The news of her death was far-reaching. Website tributes sprang up overnight, and whodunnit rumors popped up on message boards and internet chat rooms.

Police deduced that the murderer was after small things that could be pawned quickly, probably to support a drug habit. The Michael Douglas/Mel Gibson guy had been questioned and released; he'd been in Tampa at the time of the attack and was not considered a suspect. Like many other murders in New York, the death of Caroline Yates remained unsolved.

For readers and fans, the tragedy was two-fold: the death of Yates was heinous enough, compounded by the fact that the long-awaited new book penned by her had also suffered its own demise.

There were only three copies of what would have been her sixth book: one on her Hewlitt-Packard laptop, a back-up diskette stashed in her dresser, and a printed hard copy of the first draft in her study. All were destroyed by the fire.

A screeching blue jay outside the dining room window startled Anne back from New York to Michigan's upper peninsula. A cowbird answered the jay with a sneering laugh, and then a few more birds joined in the conversation. A half-dozen sparrows formed a committee on the low branch of an alder, taking roll while awaiting their turn at the feeder. A grackle blew his traffic-cop whistle. Anne looked down at the heaping piles of manuscripts on the floor.

What she needed, she decided, was a nice, cold glass of wine. Woodbridge Sauvignon Blanc, 1999, precisely. The bottle she'd purchased for a special occasion. Anne wasn't a connoisseur in the least, and certainly not, heaven forbid, a *drinker.* The last drink she'd had was last December during Allie's birthday party. A parent had brought a six-pack of Michelob, and Anne had nursed a single beer the entire evening. The bottle of wine that waited in the refrigerator had been purchased for consumption during the holidays; however, there had been no occasion to partake, and after the Christmas Eve phone call from Dr. Gardner she had been just as happy sipping hot cocoa with Allison, singing

Christmas carols, talking about dolls and *N'SYNC* and Britney Spears and waiting for Santa Claus.

She opened a kitchen drawer and trolled around for a wine opener.

"Ha, George," she said, holding up and inspecting a shiny fork. "You finally *did* get some new silverware." She was, she had to admit, disappointed to see that the rustic kitchen utensils had been replaced with more modern, up-to-date implements. The older silverware had hand-made wood handles, worn smooth from years of use. They were unique, but, one by one, failing in their age. George had replaced them with a new, more modern set, along with several other utensils. A new soup ladle, spatula set, and tongs. Even the wine opener was one of those newfangled ones, the kind with a long, nasty needle that was shoved through the cork. When a button on the handle was pressed, a compressed air cartridge forced air into the bottle and the cork popped out. Which, in theory, sounded like it might work, and probably did most of the time, unless the cork was *really in there, baby,* like the one Anne was trying to wrestle out. She didn't have much luck, and finally resorted to using the corkscrew that was one of the many tools folded within an old Swiss Army knife that, Anne was happy to find out, George hadn't replaced when he'd switched the silverware.

The first glass of Woodbridge went down surprisingly easy, during which time she'd rejected two more manuscripts, both from unpublished writers. *Killing Athena* by Jarred Morse showed a lot of promise, but it wasn't much more than a repeat knock-off of most mainstream thrillers. She did put it to the side, however, as one she would consider. Especially if the pickings were slim.

Another glass of wine. This one went down even easier than the first, and she poured another. She sipped gingerly, savoring the sweet liquid in her mouth.

"Okay, boys and girls. What's next?"

She reached down to pick up the next submission and saw Gerald Morgan's manuscript off to the side. She picked it up, smiled, then set it back down.

There is no medication in the world, she thought, shaking her head. She glanced at the bottle of Woodbridge, now dangerously close to empty. *There's not even enough of that stuff. The day Gerald Morgan gets published is the day I sing Karaoke.*

At the end of her third glass of wine she called it quits. No more reading, no more alcohol. Her body glowed and her mind buzzed from the drinks; she wasn't going to overdo it.

Well . . . I might read some more. Won't get a hangover from that.

She picked up the kitchen and organized the submissions, showered, then slipped into bed to read. The sun had finally given way to the encroaching dusk, the quivering leaves were at rest, and the murky sounds of night swallowed the forest. Crickets peeped and chimed, and an occasional bat squealed as it spun through the darkness. A quarter-sized gray moth pounded at the screen, driven mad by the single glowing light in the tiny bedroom. A few mosquitos, also entranced by the light, grasped the thin mesh wires like convicted felons.

Then—

Everything stopped. No crickets, no sounds. The night became deathly still. Anne noticed the silence, and looked up from the manuscript. It was as if a plug had been pulled, a circuit blown. There were no sounds at all, other than that silly moth battering at the screen.

Strange.

Then, one by one, the crickets began to sing. Soon, the chorus of night creatures once again blended into one perfect symphony.

Anne flipped groggily through the manuscript. The pages were heavy. The wine, coupled with the long day, had done its work. She dropped the submission to the floor beside the bed.

"Goodnight, Allie-Gator." She reached over and picked up the small stuffed animal. "She's going to be fine, isn't she?" Anne grasped the alligator's mouth and feigned its speech, pursing her lips as she spoke. "Yes, she is," Anne said in a high-pitched voice. She returned the alligator to the nightstand and clicked off the light.

"Goodnight, Allie-baby," she murmured. *"Goodni—"*

She fell asleep.

And the stalker saw it all.

ten

He had watched her read all afternoon and into the evening. He could see her on the couch, going through manuscript after manuscript. The more manuscripts she read, the angrier he became.

Why isn't she reading it?!?! his mind howled. *Why isn't she reading it?!?!?* Had she passed it by? Had she already read a bit of it and decided she didn't like it?

No. That wouldn't be the case. Once she began to read *Bestseller,* she wouldn't put it away. He was certain. He knew that once she began to read and began to see where the story was going, well . . . she'd be *hooked.*

After all, Anne . . . you're the star. You're the leading bitch.

She had opened up a bottle of wine, and he watched her as she paced the small living room, glass in one hand, manuscript in the other. Through the window he watched her lips move, and wondered if she was reading aloud. He watched her through the evening and into dusk, into nighttime. *Dark-time.* His *favorite* time. He didn't have to remain so far from the cabin, now. The blackening night would hide him well. The owner of the cabin had installed a new mercury vapor light last week; the stalker had smashed it with a rock just yesterday. It had taken one lucky throw and *smash!* Plastic and glass exploded, and the whole unit had crashed to the ground. He had been careful to pick up the broken pieces and throw them into the forest. Without the glow of the mercury light, the outside of the cottage was cloaked in icy darkness.

And when Anne had removed her clothing to shower, well, that was just an added bonus. He had crept up behind a thick, bulky spruce that grew several feet beyond the bedroom window, and peered inside as she undressed.

Annie, Annie, Annie. What lovely breasts you have. What a shapely, sexy body. The gym has served you well. You've even—

She had slipped out of the bedroom and into the tiny bathroom. He had heard the running water, the ker-*clunk* of the glass shower door closing. Heard her humming a tune. That godawful *Wind Beneath My Wings,* by Bette Midler. Puke.

Blunk. She'd dropped the soap and her humming stopped.

Did he dare? He'd have only a few minutes. He could slip inside without her knowing, and leave before she even got out of the shower.

But no. It would be too careless. He had no reason to go inside.

Not yet, anyway. But soon.

He'd heard the water stop, the chug of the glass shower door opening. Suddenly there she was, glistening wet, all naked and beautiful, toweling herself as she strode into the bedroom.

Oh, Anne.

She was facing him, towel over her face, her body fully exposed. Faint tan lines looped over her hips, rounded her breasts. Her nipples were swollen hard from the cool night air.

One hand was in his pocket, and he cupped his balls through the clothing, pulling at his scrotum.

Fuck you. Cut you. Kill you. Fuck you cut you kill you. Oh,yes. Fuck you cut you cut you kill you—

His penis was swollen and he massaged it gently, affectionately, as he watched her.

Fuck you fuck you yes oh yes fuck you cut you kill you—

He watched her climb into bed, watched her read. He continued stroking himself, faster now, pounding away, the euphoria welling up inside of him until the grip of pleasure was unbearable.

Cut you kill you fuck you cut you kill you fuck you—

His body tensed and he climaxed in silent fury, all the while watching Anne from only a few feet away.

Cut you cut you fuck you kill you kill you fuck you . . . .

He continued stroking himself long after his ejaculation, slowly, gently. His hand was sticky and wet, and he smothered the shaft of his penis with semen, breathing long sighs of exhilarating satisfaction. He smiled, his ecstacy purged. He had been quiet. Any small noise he might have made had been clouded by the singing crickets.

Oh, Anne. And it's only going to get better.

After a while, Anne had plopped the manuscript to the floor. It made a splattering *slap* on the wood.

And what the fuck was that? She's talking to a fucking toy?

She had clicked off the light beside her bed, and the stalker had slipped farther back into the shadows. Waited. He had always been amazed at how pathetically trusting people were. With all of the crime and crazy people running around, you'd think people—women, in particular—would be more careful. How many times had he been able to walk through his victim's home, unnoticed and unseen? He'd made their house his own, and it was a goddamn easy thing to do.

And what was the one bitch's name? In Miami? Christ, he'd been able to get into the home and watch her in her own house. She was reading in bed. Her husband had been sound asleep, and he watched her from the staircase for nearly an hour. When she got up to use the bathroom, he slipped downstairs and stood against a wall. If she would have turned on a light in the living room, she would have seen him. As it was, she had returned to her bedroom, crept back into bed, and picked up her book. *Lovers and Gamblers* by Jackie Collins. Shit. If she read *that* crap, she fucking *deserved* to die.

But her husband would be first. The man was sleeping on his side; he put a bullet through his back before the woman even had a clue what was going on. She screamed. They always do.

And it was always . . . *always* . . . too late.

Two hours passed. He was motionless, listening to the night sounds. Crickets, bats. An owl here or there. A few coyotes far away.

Three hours passed. Anne slept.

Three hours. That's long enough.

Quietly, cautiously, he made his way through the darkness to the door of the cabin.

eleven

Morning. Shafts of sunlight streamed through the trees. Anne opened her eyes and squinted in the morning light.

Hel-lo, she thought, recalling the wine from the night before. Her head throbbed, but not badly. There was a slight curtain of haze that swelled between her temples; nothing more.

Three glasses, Anne Harper. Looks like you better go on the wagon.

She sat up in bed. The fresh breath of morning poured through the screen, filling the small bedroom. The air was scented and sweet, blended, redolent of the aromatherapy candle shelf at Wal-Mart, only not near as strong. The chatter of birds replaced the numbing noises of the city. Anne closed her eyes and drifted with the morning.

After a few minutes she rolled to her side. The manuscript that she had been reading last night was on the floor, and she reached down and picked it up. This one was penned by yet another unpublished writer, Joseph P. Karnycki. The work was called *Silence.* It was reasonably well-written, except for one fatal flaw: it was a complete knock-off of Dean Koontz's *Lightning.* So complete of a knock-off that it didn't just border on plagiarism—it *screamed* it. Story, characters, plot, *everything.* Anne was amazed that someone would be so bold as to actually *submit* a piece such as this to a literary agent. No publisher in the world would touch it. Koontz's lawyers and those of his publisher would have a field day with this one, and they'd win.

She set the manuscript back down and her thoughts traveled, winding back to Allie. Back to sterile, white rooms. Needles and more tears and more *this won't hurt a bit*'s.

More tests. There would always be more tests.

Stop it.

We've found something, Anne. Something in one of Allie's tests. It's probably nothing.

No matter what, Anne reasoned, her daughter would be battling the monster for the rest of her life in some form or another. It was so cruel, so unfair. Often she found herself whispering a silent prayer to God, only to curse him minutes later for allowing Allie to have the disease in the first place.

What kind of a God would do that? she wondered. *What kind of a God would—*

Enough. It was pointless to sit here worrying about it, twelve hours out of New York, when she couldn't do anything about it. And even if she *was* home, there was still nothing she could do. It was, as the overused adage goes, out of her hands. She pushed the thoughts away and concentrated on the submissions she'd need to go over, glancing at Karnycki's *Silence* heaped on the floor.

Why is everyone trying to copy everyone else's style? she wondered. Sure, writers do their homework. They know what is selling. They read the top-sellers, figure that *those* authors must be doing something right, and attempt to develop their own version of the heavies like John Grisham or Patricia Cornwell or Clive Cussler or Stephen King. And if she received one more note from a writer claiming that his or her story was a cross between *so-and-so* and *so-and-so*, it was going straight to the round file. Sayanara, baby. She'd really been hoping that she'd see some original, unique stuff—but it was becoming less and less frequent. Damn near nonexistent, in fact.

The fact was, over the past several years, a growing number of authors were becoming increasingly frustrated with their publishers and agents. Many authors were opting to self-publish, to cut out the middlemen. More and more writers were becoming successful at it, too—sometimes making ten times the money than they would from even some of the larger publishing houses. Fifteen years ago, that would have been unthinkable. In the eighties, when the self-publishing phenomenon really began to grow, the big publishers laughed and thumbed their noses. Now, however, it was a different story.

Stewart Harding had been a literary boy-wonder for nearly a decade. He was under contract with one of the largest publishers in the country, and he churned out two and sometimes three top-selling novels each year. When Harding left his publisher to self-publish on his own, everyone thought he was mad. He was belittled in the trades, and was the brunt of jokes at the stuffy New York parties. Why would millionaire author Stewart Harding leave behind his deal to—heaven forbid—*self-publish?*

Of course, that was then, this was now. Within three years, it wasn't Stewart Harding, millionaire author. It was Stewart Harding, *billionaire* author . . . and publisher. His success was unprecedented. Every single book he had written and self-published went on to be a number-one seller, often dominating the top spot for months. Harding even wrote a book on self-publishing that was still a top ten nonfiction bestseller.

Following Harding's lead, other successful authors had jumped onto the self-publishing bandwagon. It was a new world with new possibilities, without all the bullshit from the biggies. Self-publishing was, by no means, a get-rich-quick scheme. Anyone with a computer and a few thousand dollars could pump out five thousand copies of their masterpiece, but it was the marketing that so many entrepreneurs neglected. Many authors failed miserably, and wound up with several thousand token Christmas gifts that would remain in their basement next to the rotting treadmill and the hardly-used stationary bicycle.

But the fact remained that, in the age of laptops and personal computers the size of wallets, of decent color printers that could be bought at Office Max or Staples or Sam's Club for under two hundred dollars, today's writer had *far* more options than he or she ever had before. Which, in Anne's business, made the pickings slimmer and slimmer every year. She'd already lost two clients to the self-publishing wheel of fortune; she didn't want to lose any more. The bigger publishers were going to have to change a few things if they wanted to survive. And if *they* didn't survive, well, then . . . .

She pulled the covers back, swung her legs to the floor, and paused. Yawned. Smiled when she saw the toothy reptile still seated at its post.

"G'mornin', Allie-Gator," she said to the gaping beanie baby. Anne stood up, slipped into an over-sized T-shirt, and walked into the kitchen.

A thin glaze of fog slithered over the lake like a smoky snake. The trees were comatose; not a single leaf fluttered, not a branch trembled. A chipmunk stole across a log near the water, its furry cheeks comically puffy and bloated, gorged with food. Just beyond the kitchen window, several birds were battling for positions at the feeder. When they saw the large shape looming behind the open screen they fled, screaming and screeching, into the forest.

She placed a mug of water in the microwave, set the timer for sixty seconds, and pressed the start button. The appliance hummed to life and she opened the cupboard and pulled down a box of Bigelow tea. The sampler box. She'd picked it up, along with a few other items, before she left New York.

Beep . . . beep . . . beep. The microwave stopped humming, and Anne popped the door and retrieved the steaming cup of water. She'd settled on the blackberry tea, the one that, according to the box, held a *deliciously robust blackberry flavor for those special moments you wish to cherish!*

Whatever.

She cupped the hot mug with both hands, and sipped. Outside, a chickadee sat at the feeder, snatching up seeds, warily watching the figure only a few feet away in the cabin.

The sun had risen over the trees, and a bright glare reflected from the windshield of the BMW. The car was filthy, but there wasn't much she could do about that. Not after traveling mile after mile of dirt roads.

She turned around and gazed at the lake. The water was smooth and flat, except for several tiny rings that formed here and there, probably from fish feeding at the surface.

She lowered her gaze to the table and was about to take a sip of tea when she suddenly stopped, holding the steaming mug just below her lips. She stared down at the table.

What in the hell?

twelve

The manuscript.

Bestseller was placed on the table's only placemat. The envelope was missing, and the inch-thick stack of paper sat alone, cover page staring back at her.

Bestseller, by Gerald Morgan.

How did—

She scanned the room. All of the other manuscripts were stacked neatly on or near the couch, right where she had placed them. She remembered shuffling things around last night and putting things in order before she went to bed. And she vaguely recalled picking up a manuscript and placing it on the table. But she thought it was—

No. I was tired. And the wine. I picked up the wrong manuscript, that's all.

She picked up Gerald Morgan's submission. He had certainly got her attention, especially with a story line like—well, like

your setting and scenario as the basis for BESTSELLER. I hope you enjoy it.

It was an amusing ploy to get her attention, and, for the most part, it had worked.

But again—it was Gerald Morgan, for crying out loud. The one she'd had arrested for trashing her office and nearly assaulting Candace. Gerald Morgan, the schizo that had sent her one awful manuscript after another, each one worse than the previous. And now—

Bestseller.

More mindless drivel from a raging looney-toon, Anne thought. She returned the manuscript to the table, sat down, and turned the cover page over. There was only a small paragraph on the first page. It read:

The following is a work of fiction. Names, places, characters and incidents are products of the author's imagination, or are used fictitiously. Any resemblance to any person, living or dead, is purely coincidental. This is an original work by Gerald R.

Morgan. PO Box 4252, White Plains, NY 20042. (202) 555-2376

Right beneath the typewritten legal notice, Morgan had scribbled in blue ink:

It's only a story, Ms. Harper. Happy reading! —GM

Anne smiled, shook her head. Sipped her tea. Glanced out the window, then back at the manuscript. Smiled again.

Crazy Gerald.

She turned the legal page face down on the table, and began to read.

thirteen

From where he was hidden, the stalker had a clear view of the cabin. He was cramped and uncomfortable from being in the same position most of the night, but now it was worth it. He saw Anne at the table, saw her sipping tea, saw her reading—and he *knew*. He knew she was reading *Bestseller*. He smiled, giddy with excitement.

It had been simple to slip silently into the cabin during the night. The door was left wide open, and the screen door only had a hook latch. The stalker never even made a sound. He'd found the manuscript on the floor and placed it on the table where she would be certain to find it. It had been even easier since she'd already arranged a manuscript on the table; all he had to do was replace it with *Bestseller*. Which was good.

He didn't want to arouse too much suspicion. Not just yet. Not this early in the game.

There's still lots of fun to be had, Annie. Don't want to scare you off just yet.

Through the dining room window, he saw her turn a page.

Good. Just getting started.

He was dying to know what was going through her mind. After all, the story, he felt, *was* very well written. It's original; that's what she liked. It said so in the *Literary Agent Handbook*. Page 67, paragraph three, listed *The Anne Harper Agency*. Submission requirements, address, phone number, fax, e-mail. And in the 'special additions' section: '. . . *looking for fresh, original approaches. Psychological suspense/thrillers only. Remember: great ideas are everywhere; try and make your story different.'*

He smiled again.

Well, it's different, alright, Anne. Certainly original. You have to like it, Annie Harper. It's got a killer of an ending, if ya knowwhuttamean, Vern. Besides . . . it has 'bestseller' written all over it.

He continued watching her. His ego swelled, his narcissistic pride raged.

And somewhere, hatred and anger burned.

A whore for the masses, that's what you are. A bookslut. You and everyone you're in bed with. He mentally ridiculed the entire publishing industry. Everyone in the book business thought they were so fucking smart. The publishers thrived, while they fed their authors bits and scraps. Not the big guys, not the John Sauls or the Tom Clancys or the Danielle Steeles. They made shitloads of money. Sure, they were being taken advantage of, like every other writer hooked up with a big pimp. But at least *some* of the big names were making *some* money.

But, by far and large, it was the *other people* who were making the money. Everybody had their greedy, grubby hands in the pie. The editors, the agents, the consultants, the printers, the publishers, right on down to the distributors. If there was any money left after they received *their* share, then, and only then, would a tiny bone be tossed to the lowly author. And of course, the author would lunge at the minuscule portion like a housefly on fresh dog shit. They had no choice. Do what the publisher says, write what we want you to write. Sit, Rex, sit. Fetch, boy. And bend over while you're at it.

And he was sick of being rejected, time and time again. Manuscript after manuscript, submission after submission, all returned with the standard, scripted rejection letter. *'Although your work is intriguing, we do not feel, at this time, that it is right for us. Opinions, however, vary greatly, and you may well find success with another agent or publisher.'*

It was New York language for *you suck, your writing sucks, and don't bother us anymore with your nonsensical waste of paper and ink.*

But this time, *he* was going to have the last word. The final say, the final chapter. He was going to kill one of the top literary agents in the country. Anne Harper, Golden Girl of the Book Biz. Anne Harper, with all the big names, all the connections, all the big clients. Anne Harper, whose husband just happened to get caught banging the sixteen year-old babysitter a few years ago, causing a very messy and *very* public divorce. And how the slimeball remained out of prison for *that* one hadn't been a dime-store mystery: Chad Harper had money, and he bought himself a misdemeanor and short probation. He continued his work as a lawyer in DC, and was probably fucking his secretary.

Now, someone else was going to do the fucking for a change. For a change, someone *else* was going to feel like he did. Someone *else* was going to squirm and wriggle and beg.

Anne Harper. He wanted her to feel scared, wanted to see the terror in her eyes and on her face. And it was going to be messy, just like they *all* were. Messy, messy *messy*. He wanted to see the blood slowly run from a small incision, wanted to watch her bleed like he'd been bleeding for years.

And I'm just the guy to do it, he thought. *After all . . . I'm just going by the book, Anne. Just going by the book.*

fourteen

Anne finished the first six chapters of *Bestseller* and looked out the window.

Surprise, surprise, she thought. *Bestseller* was actually quite good. She liked what she'd read so far, and she'd read more than she'd intended. It was definitely different. A bit wordy in places, but that could be corrected by a good editor. Several pages were a bit odd and seemed like they didn't quite fit, but, again, a copyeditor would take care of that. The typewritten text was blotchy and splattered in many places, but that's to be expected from an old manual typewriter. Anne guessed that Morgan probably couldn't afford a computer, even a used one. No matter. If the story was good, she could work with whatever media necessary.

She was disturbed, however, about the tact that Morgan used. A story about a literary agent being stalked at a remote cabin was a bit unnerving, considering her circumstances. But the ploy worked. Morgan wanted to write something that would get her attention; he'd succeeded. His sentence structure, grammar . . . even his spelling was much better than his previous submissions.

And yet, it was the certain parallels he'd written into the story that caused Anne to pause and re-read a sentence or paragraph. In *Bestseller,* the cabin where Beth Huston was staying is described in great detail, and it mimicked the very cabin Anne was staying in. Not *perfectly,* but there were certain similarities. The lake in the story is about the same size as Lost Lake, only Morgan had named it Loon Lake. To reach the cabin it was necessary to travel a

sparsely traveled dirt road, followed by several miles of even less-traveled two-track. The journey was bumpy and rugged, and the car winced with every jolt.

But again: Anne was impressed with what she read. Morgan's concept of creating the story in such fashion was an interesting idea. And his writing, by her own assessment, had improved dramatically.

Hope that medicine holds out for the rest of the book, she thought. If Gerald Morgan was on medication to keep him on an even keel, terrific. If it helped to make him a better writer, well, that was just an added bonus. She flipped back to the legal page and read Morgan's hand-scrawled note to her.

It's only a story, Ms. Harper. Happy reading! —GM

She turned the pages back over and marked the spot where she had left off, still surprised that she'd read as far as she did.

Gerald Morgan. Wait 'till Candace hears this.

She stood up, stretched, and walked into the bedroom. Anne knelt at the nightstand and pursed her lips.

"How are you doing in here, Allie-Gator?" Baby-talk. "Glad to be out of the city for a while?" she asked, petting the creature that stood guard. The reptile dutifully ignored her and continued his watch. Anne slipped into a pair of shorts, decided that the T-shirt she was already wearing would suffice, and left the cabin.

The dock was warm beneath her bare feet. It was nearing noon, and the temperature had risen considerably since earlier in the morning. Tiny water creatures—minnows, small crayfish, waterbugs—recoiled at the site of the giant shadow that swept over them. Skitterbugs spun in mad circles on the surface. High above, the Creator had been careless with his cotton swabs again; he'd spilled them all over his bright blue linoleum floor. Several ducks honked as they sped by, their wings whistling like teakettles. They skidded on webbed wheels to the surface, landing near the middle of the lake.

Anne turned her head as she walked, noticing a rather large cedar that—

A large cedar?

—that bowed out over the water and spread its branches—

Like a billowing green canopy?

—like a billowing green canopy over the water. She stopped and stared at the tall, leafy tree. She'd read about this tree. She'd read about it in Morgan's book. An enormous cedar, not far from the dock. The words from *Bestseller* came to her. In Morgan's story

Beth turned her head as she walked, noticing a rather large cedar that bowed out above the water and spread its branches like a billowing green canopy.

Anne turned around and looked at the cabin that sat

serene and comfortable on the shore, while birds feasted at the various feeders placed around the small, shaded yard.

She shook her head and smiled. *Right on, Morgan,* she thought. The book was alive, and the details were all around her. Then—

Had he been here? Was it possible that he actually came here, knew of this place?

It was possible, but highly unlikely. Sure, many people knew that she traveled to a remote cabin in the wilds of

Michigan's upper peninsula. Few people, however, knew exactly *where.* And even if they did, well, good luck trying to find it. Two-track roads spider-webbed across thousands of acres in Michigan's upper peninsula. There were hundreds of lakes; three others within a few hundred square miles that were called 'Lost Lake'.

She looked around. Thick trees grew cramped and tight to the shoreline, and the tops of cedar trees poked at the sky like tribal lances. There were no beaches, no meadows or fields. The thick forest butted right up to the waters' edge, except, of course, across the lake where the only other cabin was.

In surveying her surroundings, she found several other large cedars that would have fit the description of the one not far from the dock. She was being paranoid . . . and she *liked* that. *Bestseller* was making her think. When a book stays with you after you've put it down, the writer has done their job. A good portion of their job, anyway.

At the end of the dock, a school of inch-long minnows clouded the water. The entire swarm flinched in horror as the shadow swept over them. Here the water was deeper, maybe to a depth of six feet or so. Anne remembered swimming and not being able to touch her toes until mid-way along the dock. She contemplated a plunge into the icy waters. It would be cold, alright. She reached down and swished her hand into the water.

Anne Harper, you big chicken. Fifteen years ago you would have sailed off this dock. She smiled.

Not today.

She stood up, dried her hand on her shirt, and stopped.

A noise. She'd heard a noise in the woods, near the big cedar.

Anne froze.

fifteen

As he watched her walk along the dock, he could almost feel her uneasiness.

She's reading, alright, he thought. *No doubt about it.*

He watched her stop part way along the dock and notice the big cedar tree. It was, after all, just like the book. He was pleased to no end to see her stop and pause.

And her face.

The sun was pouring down, and her cheeks were lightly bronzed. He admired her profile, the outline of her body, the tanned skin of her legs. The stalker knew he was taking a big risk by hiding beneath the overturned rowboat, but now he was *glad.* He'd waited there all night, constricted and confined, battling mosquitos and biting flies and the cold, wet ground. Now it was worth it. He was so close. So close he could almost—

Touch her. Yes, that would—that will—*be wonderful.*

She had continued to the end of the dock, and he used the opportunity to shift and try to get more comfortable. His calf developed a cramp, paralyzing his leg below his knee. It had been painful; now it was simply numb.

When he peeked out again she was at the end of the dock, absently swishing the water with her hand. Then she stood up, began to dry her hand on her shirt, and stopped. She again turned her attention toward the large cedar tree.

The stalker had heard the noise, too. A branch snapping. Ever so light and subtle. He shifted carefully beneath the boat to see where the noise had come from.

Anne was at the end of the dock, unmoving. She was looking at something. Her hand was raised to her forehead in salute, shading her eyes from the sun. She was looking at something, for sure. Or looking *for* something. He couldn't tell.

He twisted on the wet ground beneath the rowboat, and heard another snap. Louder this time. He froze, watching Anne watching.

Something was moving. He could hear it now, crunching through brush. Something perhaps sixty or seventy feet away. But what? Who? The old guy from across the lake? What would he be doing here?

Again, he shifted to try and peer through a slim crack to see what held Anne's attention.

No, not the old guy. They'd be talking. He'd hear voices. It frustrated him that he could only see Anne, and she was still standing at the end of the dock, her attention drawn to the huge cedar tree.

sixteen

Anne remained motionless, thumb to her forehead, palm flat. Not a single muscle twitched. She kept absolutely still.

The deer had peeked around the cedar tree, guarded, wary. Anne had spotted its head as it inspected the shoreline. Then, the animal slunk out into the open, cautiously watchful as it bent down to drink. It was skittish, cagey.

Anne watched, transfixed. The creature was beautiful. Sure, she'd seen deer before. Certainly not in New York City, of all places. But farther north, in the Catskills. She'd seen quite a few there, and other parts of upstate New York. And here, of course. There were deer all over Michigan's upper peninsula, to the point of creating environmental problems. Here, the deer population had reached an all-time high, and in many areas, there just wasn't enough habitat to support the herd. Evidence of their overpopulation was everywhere, most notably on the rural highways, where their dead carcasses were often spotted on the shoulder, the victims of a fast-moving car or truck.

But she'd never been so *close* to one before. Not in the wild, not like this. The animal looked so gentle and delicate. Big brown eyes flashed nervously about as it lapped at the water, and its ears fluttered occasionally.

Anne didn't breath. She was afraid the animal would hear her breathing, or see a slight movement of her chest if she drew even the tiniest breath. She didn't blink.

Oh, Allie. I wish you were here, sweetheart. I wish you could see this.

Next year.

Suddenly, the deer raised its head. The animal froze, stiff and rigid, staring toward the cabin. Its eyes were focused, ears up and alert. Anne followed its gaze without moving her head. The deer had been spooked by something.

Seconds passed. Animal and human were locked, still and unmoving. Anne traded glances from the deer to the cabin, back to the deer, then to the yard and the rowboat overturned on shore. Back to the deer, then back to the cabin.

Without warning, the deer bolted. In a swift instant it had pivoted back around and leapt away. Anne caught a flash of brown, a sliver of white tail, and the creature had vanished.

She heard it crashing away, the sounds of its escape fading off into the forest. The deer was gone.

Anne was elated and she looked around, gazing at the pristine sky, the green trees, the water.

And she was glad she came. Maybe everyone was right. Maybe she really *did* need some time away. Sure, she missed Allie, and had she not been able to leave her with Marta, she would have never left. But Marta was good. Kind and gentle. Allie adored Marta, or 'Aunt Mimi' as she called her. She imagined that the two of them, at this very moment, were either snuggled together on the couch reading *Charlotte's Web* for the umpteenth time. Or *Little House on the Prarie.* Or perhaps they were out walking, or at the playground.

And today was Sunday. Matinee day, the day Anne and Allie would see a movie together. Today, in her absence, Marta had promised to take Allison to a show. Anne would travel to Three Corners this evening to call and find out what she'd missed at the matinee. Allie was sure to give her the play-by-play of the entire movie, and Anne would listen, smiling, for however long it took. Anne would tell her about the deer and the hummingbirds and the big crayfish.

Next year, Allie. Promise. And I won't even think *about fishing without you.*

She scanned the yard, and her eyes stopped on the rowboat.

Now, there's an idea, she thought, and began walking along the dock back to shore.

seventeen

When he heard the noise, the sudden crashing through the forest, he knew immediately what it was. He'd spotted many deer here before. Lots of them. He'd almost hit one with the car just last week, for crying out loud. And during a walk through the woods two days ago, he'd surprised a sleeping buck, scaring the shit out of both of them. The animal had leapt to its feet, snorting madly as it bounded off. He wasn't sure who had been more surprised: he or the deer.

He watched Anne walk along the dock, and he heard her bare feet plodding on the old wooden planks. He heard the swishing of grass when she stepped from the dock to the shore.

But—

Something was wrong. Something wasn't going according to plan.

The swishing of grass was getting *louder.* She was coming *closer.*

No, no, no, he thought. *No! Not now!* The prospect of being discovered enraged him. *Not yet! No! Not yet! You're going to fuck everything up!*

He squirmed gently beneath the boat, feeling for the knife in its sheath. He pulled it out swiftly, silently, and gripped it tightly. Her footsteps drew nearer. Unfortunately, the game was over. Things weren't going to go as planned, after all.

And his disappointment was *immeasurable.* This was not the way it was written, not what he had planned. He wanted her to read the story, to *slowly* put two-and-two together, wanted to watch her terror grow until the last second when she'd had enough—but by then it would be too late.

But she hadn't read enough. Things were fucked up. Not *completely,* not *totally.* He'd have to jump to the end of the book, that's all, and miss the fun in between. Now, he had some quick decisions to make.

She'll lift the boat up. When she does, I'll slice her feet, just above the ankles. That'll drop her like a fucking rock, but it won't kill her. Don't want to do that just yet.

The swishing drew nearer, and his heart slammed in his chest. He flexed his grip around the knife handle, ready. Flex, release, flex, release.

Closer . . . .

He held his breath.

Flex, release, flex. He squeezed the knife so hard that his fingernails dug into his palm, causing his hand to bleed.

Flex. Release. *Flex* . . . .

A pair of fingers appeared, and two bare feet, visible only part-way to her knee. Hands grasped the gunwhale of the boat, mere inches from his face.

His hand tightened around the knife handle.

The ankles. When she lifts the boat . . . .

He twisted his arm, turning the blade outward. He pulled it to his chest, moments away from striking.

Sorry, Anne. This would have been so much more fun if you had played it by the book. You have no idea how awful this makes me feel.

eighteen

"Oh shit. Forgot."

Anne released her grip on the edge of the boat and stood up straight. She'd need the oars, of course. George Otto kept them in the shed. She turned and walked to the small building at the far edge of the yard.

The door was locked, but the key was right where it always was: beneath the rusted kerosene lantern that sat on a graying cedar post several feet from the shed. The heavy padlock popped open, and she returned the key to its proper place beneath the old lantern. The inside of the shed was filled with odds and ends: tools, hardware, and the like. An old push mower sat in the corner like the skeleton of a dinosaur. On the walls, various hand tools hung, most of them old, probably antiques. Yet George still used them all. He felt they were worth more to him here at the cabin than they would be in his wallet.

The oars were on the wall, too, resting on four-inch nails. They were old and gray, and the wood was bowed and unfinished with a driftwood quality about them. At one time they had been painted green, as evident by the few remaining flecks that clung to the wood. The finish had long worn off, but the lumber was solid.

Anne lifted the oars from the wall and leaned them against the outside of the shed. She closed the door, returned the padlock to its place, but didn't lock it.

Then she had another idea. She carried the oars to the rowboat, laid them down on the grass, and walked back into the cabin. There were still nearly two dozen manuscripts that she hadn't touched; she'd take a few with her on the boat.

And a sandwich. Now you're thinking, Annie girl. Lunch on the lake.

Pickings were slim in the sandwich department. She hadn't been to the General Store in Three Corners yet, so she only had the most basic of basics: bread and peanut butter. That would have to do. A peanut butter sandwich and a bottle of *Evian,* to be enjoyed in an old rowboat on a beautiful, pristine lake. If she wouldn't quite be in heaven, she'd certainly be in the waiting room.

The sun shined down, and millions of flashbulbs popped on and off on the surface of the lake. A gentle breeze played with her bangs and rocked the boat ever so gently. She drifted lazily, read a bit, then looked around, read a bit more, looked around again. She continued to marvel at the beauty all around her.

To the south, a pair of loons had been fishing near the shore. She placed the three manuscripts she'd brought (*Night of Fear,* by Emilio Sanchez, *Whirlwind,* by Gabriella Donaldson, and *For These Eyes,* by Jeremy Seeger. Seeger's work showed some promise, and she made a mental note to continue with this one) and began to row toward the loons to see how close she could actually get to them.

To the east, on the other side of the lake, the cabin sat in the shade of the pines.

And the stalker was inside.

nineteen

It had been a close one.

He had been seconds—mere *seconds*—from slashing her ankles. But at the last moment the fingers disappeared and he heard her feet swishing off through the grass.

Atta girl, Annie. You're playing like a real trouper now.

Peering out from beneath the boat, he had waited until she entered the shed. When she was out of sight, he slipped out from beneath the overturned rowboat. He slunk across the grass to the other side of the cabin and skulked quietly, unseen, into the woods.

But that had been close. *Too* close. He had been careless, and he had nearly blown it.

From the forest, he watched her carry the oars to the boat, then go back into the cabin. He couldn't see what she was doing, but he could see her silhouette moving about in the kitchen. He was just about to move to a better viewing point when she emerged from the cabin carrying a small brown bag and several large envelopes. She carried them to the dock, overturned and launched the rowboat. She brought it up alongside the dock, gathered up the manuscripts and the brown bag, and rowed slowly out into the lake.

Oh, perfect, Anne. Perfect. You must be reading ahead. You must be enjoying what you're reading.

When she had rowed a good distance out into the lake, he emerged from the forest, walked quickly to the cabin, and went inside.

A bottle of wine, nearly empty, sat on the counter. An empty coffee mug, upside down, sat in a gaudy blue dish strainer in the sink.

"Thanks, Anne," he said aloud. "Don't mind if I do. You're a gracious host." He picked up the mug and filled it with cold water from the sink. He drank slowly, easily, then sat the mug back on the strainer, upside down.

Manuscripts were towered on the floor near the couch. On the table was *Bestseller,* face up, at chapter seven.

"That's good, Anne," he whispered. He was pleased; she'd read more than he'd expected. He flipped through the first few chapters to see if she'd made any notes. Nothing much. A few corrections, an improper word here and there. She'd 'x'd out a few paragraphs, underlined some sentences. He was careful to leave the pages as they were.

To the bedroom. He knew his way around the cabin well, as he'd been here a dozen times in the past few weeks. It had been a cinch to watch the owner pick up a rock, retrieve a key, and open the door. He now had the run of the place—any time he wanted.

The bedroom was tidy. The bed was made, and there was some stupid fucking stuffed animal on the nightstand. He picked it up and inspected it, then placed it back down.

You're going to need a little more than pet alligators to save your ass, Anne, he thought.

The dresser, top drawer first.

Bingo.

He perused her panties, lovingly fingering the fine fabric. One particular pair he held to his cheek, caressing his face with the soft, silky material. Over and over, across his lips, flicking his tongue out and tasting the dryness. Slowly, gently, down his neck. He slipped his hand inside his shirt and gently brushed his nipples with the supple cloth, unbuttoning his camouflage pants with his free hand.

And it was *exquisite.*

Five minutes later, after composing himself and stuffing the soiled panties in his pocket, he turned and left the bedroom. Through the dining room window, he saw the rowboat in the lake.

Good, Anne. Take your time.

He walked into the bathroom. Next to the shower stall was a door made of knotty pine. It blended in to the walls of the room, except for a small, clear plastic door handle. He opened it up, wriggled inside, and closed the door behind him.

twenty

She had been able to get surprisingly close to the loons before they became alarmed and headed out into deeper water. At the shoreline, a stream flowed into the lake, and Anne guessed that this was an area where a lot of fish were, hence, good hunting grounds for the loons. After the loons fled she rowed back to the cabin and left the boat moored at the dock. She'd be using it again; might as well leave it tied and ready.

Three o'clock. Inside the cabin, she placed the three manuscripts on the floor in a neat pile. Then, as an afterthought, she pulled out *For These Eyes* by Jeremy Seeger. There was some good stuff there. Certainly better than most of the hum-drum material she'd come across so far.

She arranged the manuscripts in an orderly fashion on the floor around the fireplace. The *haven't got to these yet* pile sat on the stone hearth next to a small stack of birch logs (this was by *far* the largest pile). The definite *'nos'* went on the mantle next to the old *Cobra* CB radio. The *long shot maybe if you do a lot of rewrites* manuscripts were placed in a pile in front of the brass fireplace tongs, the *better have another looks* were arranged in front of the couch, the *hey this isn't bads* on a foot stool (This consisted of Seeger's *For These Eyes;* none others) and the *I think this is pretty good stuff* sat on the table. There was only one manuscript in that pile, too. Everything had its place.

But then, there was Anne and Allie's scrapbook.

She took it with her everywhere, and Anne knew the ritual probably went to ridiculous lengths. If she was only going out of town for one night, she took the scrapbook. Couple hours? Take the scrapbook. Most parents kept photos of their kids in their wallets. Annie kept her photos in a hand-bound work that was thicker than Tolstoy's *War and Peace.* Heavier, too. A *lot* heavier.

The cover was made of blue construction paper. Laminated. Allie had drawn a duck on the front in red crayon, but it had faded since last year. Repeated handling of the homemade book had required some major repairs, but now the spine was solidly intact, thanks to the miracle of duct tape and staples.

And inside . . . .

Photographs. *Dozens.* Pictures and notes.

Anne sat down at the table and flipped it open. It was a silly habit, she had always thought, and was borderline neurotic. *How many parents create a scrapbook with their kid, only to find that they can't live without it? Jesus. I take this thing everywhere. How many parents do that?*

One parent, for sure. Probably more.

Being away from Allie from time to time was necessary in her business. And probably good, too, now that Allie was getting older. She was okay; she'd gotten better. She was healthy, knock wood.

But Anne had promised herself. She'd promised Allie.

Nothing for granted, sweetie. Nothing. Ever again.

Most of the pictures in the book were taken at the hospital, at Mayo Clinic, when Allie was sick. The first photo was a picture of mother and daughter snuggled together in a hospital bed, all smiles. The early days, the hot dog-and-marshmallow days, as Anne called them.

Next was Allie and a clown. Allie looked tired, worn down. The clown was showing her how to make balloon animals. A local Kiwanis group sponsored hospital visits for kids, complete with games, clowns, free stuffed animals, books, and . . . *laughter.* Lots and lots of laughter. It was needed.

Anne flipped to the center of the scrapbook. Tears welled up.

The Dark Days.

The photo was Allie and herself, seated side by side, on the bed.

Bald. Both of them.

The radiation treatments had caused Allie to lose all of her hair. She was devastated, and didn't understand. How could she? She was seven years old, for chrisssake. *How come it's comin' out, Mommy? How come? What's happening to me?*

Anne, seeing her daughter in the confused bewilderment of such a loss, walked into the hospital bathroom, cut whatever hair she could with the scissors from her purse, then shaved the rest with a razor that she'd found in the medicine cabinet. The resulting photo was taken by a nurse who, so moved by the gesture, burst into tears after taking the picture, and had to leave the room.

But the photo was *golden.* Despite the pain, the trauma and the trials little Allie was going through, Anne had never seen a bigger, more satisfied smile on her daughter.

Bald? That's okay. My mommy doesn't have hair anymore, and it seems okay-fine with her. In the picture, the two sat, arm in arm on the bed, facing the camera. Anne was a mess; she knew what the situation incurred. She was newly bald, emotionally drained, and she looked *awful.* Purple saddles drooped beneath her glazed, tired eyes. But her disorder was *cosmetic.* She couldn't have cared less. The hair would grow back. The puffiness beneath her eyes would go away.

Allie, on the other hand, looked pale, thin, and gaunt. She was a tiny girl as it was, but now she'd lost twenty pounds—more than a third of her weight—and her bones showed through her bleached, sallow skin.

But her *smile.* Her happy glow was precious, pure *platinum.* Allie's dimpled grin would have short-circuited the camera on the space shuttle. You would have been able to see the sparks from earth.

Snap. Pop. We've got a picture of little Allie, Houston. She just fried our electronics. Advise?

Roger that, shuttle. Shave your heads, and remember what you're here for.

Copy that, Houston. Shaving heads and taking pictures. Requesting permission to make a scrapbook.

Permission granted. Make the scrapbook. And be sure to use duct tape. That shit lasts forever.

Anne put the scrapbook down. She was finally to the point where she could flip through the pages and not turn into a blubbering neanderthal. Not that it would have bothered her if she had. But the scrapbook was her ritual. Some people meditated, some people prayed. Others hummed mantras while seated in a contorted yoga position. Still more lit candles at church, or fingered rosary beads while repeating Hail Marys. That was all fine. Anne Harper flipped through a scrapbook. It was *real.* It was *tangible.* It was *Allie.* Allie was alive, after all the smoke cleared, after all the drugs and chemo and sleepless nights. After all the bullshit.

Never again, baby. Never again. I love you, honey. More than you'll ever know.

twenty one

What in the fuck is she doing?

He watched her flip open the big blue book, but from where he was, he couldn't see the contents. And he was only ten feet away, for crying out loud.

He'd found the water heater closet a week ago, long before Anne arrived. The door opened up in the hallway, but the area containing the apparatus was much larger than it needed to be. It looked as if it had been built for a water heater that was much larger than the seventy-five gallon unit it contained. The result was a good-sized space behind the heater. The crevice between the drum and the wall was thin, but he had managed. Once he positioned himself between the wall and the large white cylinder, he could remain hidden indefinitely.

And the knothole . . . .

When he'd first entered the room last week and closed the door, light shined through several knotholes that were loose. The first one, directly in front of him, had popped out quite easily with only a bit of prodding with his finger. The small hole was virtually unnoticeable from the hall or anywhere else in the cabin, and it gave him a view of the living and dining area, part of the kitchen, and the hall.

The other knothole was in the closet door itself. There was already a quarter of an inch opening. It was on the other side of the hot water heater and did not provide much of a view. He could glimpse part of the toilet, the sink, and the mirror. True, he could have whittled away at the hole and made it larger, but that would be unnecessary. No, what he had right now was just *fine.*

But right now, he couldn't figure out what in the hell she was doing. She'd been poring over the blue book for nearly an hour, while all of the manuscripts sat in their neatly arranged piles.

And what is that? A tear? What's she reading? Old Yeller?

The more he watched her, the more enraged he became.

It's right on the fucking table, he thought. *Pick it up! What in the hell is so goddamn important in that blue book?!?!*

He stood in the enclosed darkness, boiling. He hated the waiting. Oh, his patience was fine. Saintly, even. But only on *his* terms. He knew when he'd have to wait, and he was prepared for it.

But when someone made *him* wait, when he waited on someone *else's* terms, well, then, look out. *That* was a kind of wait that he didn't have the patience for.

And right now, his patience was running out. The water tank two inches in front of him was full to the top, but his patience had all but dried up. It was at the bottom of the well.

His heart was beating faster. He clenched and unclenched his fists, re-opening the wounds he'd caused when he was under the boat, digging his nails into his palms. Now, however, he squeezed even harder, causing the small cuts to bleed profusely. The warm droplets oozed from his hand and silently fell to the wood floor. This, however, was not something he was aware of. He was only aware of his soaring anger, his mad rage, the pitching and flailing of his heart.

Get control, he ordered himself. *Quit fucking around. Calm down. Calm—*

A bead of sweat trickled down the bridge of his nose, and he raised his hand to wipe it away. His hand bumped something on the hot water heater and there was a noticeable, metallic *ping.*

He froze, and peered out the small knothole into the living room where Anne sat, cross-legged, on the floor.

The big blue book was open in her lap. She, too, was still, and her head was raised.

She was looking right at him.

twenty two

It wasn't loud. It was just a scrape of some sort, like something striking metal. Muffled, though.

She sat silently for a moment, her gaze fixed on the hall. Her eyes scanned the open bedroom door, then the open bathroom door. She watched the hall. She listened, but didn't hear anything more.

Still—

Anne placed the scrapbook on the floor and stood up. A long curl of hair fell in front of her face and she pulled it back with one finger, looping it behind her ear. She couldn't be sure exactly where the noise came from. The bathroom, perhaps. Possibly the bedroom. Either of the two.

She walked down the hall and into the bedroom. Allie-Gator sat on the nightstand. He reported no offenses. Everything was in order, except the top drawer of her dresser was open. She walked to it, closed it, and proceeded to the bathroom.

Nothing. *Except—*

Lipstick. A bronze cannister of lipstick lay on the floor beneath the sink. She picked it up and looked in the mirror, smiling. She shook her head.

"Okay, Morgan," she said aloud. "Stop it. Your story is freaking me out." Another smile.

That was *good,* and she *knew* it. She'd forced herself to stay away from the manuscript, and that was a *good* thing. She'd only felt that way a few other times in her career, and she liked it. *All* of Caroline Yates's manuscripts had made her feel that way, of course. And Mark Franklin's first book, too. Randy Goldman's book, *Insatiable Passion,* made her climb the walls.

Randy Goldman was another one of her very first clients, and was *certifiably* insane. A complete madman, and she'd told him this on a number of occasions. He seemed to relish in the moniker, but Anne wasn't joking. Randy Goldman was a man, she thought, that could snap at any moment. Some of the things he'd written were so twisted, so sickeningly bizarre that she couldn't stand to read them. But she *did.* He *made* her read them. It was all in how he told the story, how he put it together. Goldman even insisted on doing his own editing, which Anne was adamantly opposed to. But Goldman got his way. *Fine, Anne,* he had said. *But if someone else other than me edits this book, you can kiss any future books goodbye.*

Goldman edited his own book.

A year later, Goldman ditched her to delve into the self-publishing mine. She was *furious.* She had worked so hard for him. He was a social invalid who couldn't negotiate a loan for a box of donuts, and she had gone to bat for him to make sure he wasn't taken advantage of, made sure that he got a fair deal. The usual stuff, the stuff a good agent is supposed to do. She'd pressured the publisher to make sure they paid the advance and royalties on time. The Anne Harper Agency had gone way out on a limb for him more than once, simply so Goldman got what he wanted. How he could leave her hanging to do something so . . . *irresponsible* . . . was beyond her capacity to reason. Beyond *anyone's* capacity to reason. However, the self-publishing mine hadn't yet been kind to Goldman, and he hadn't fared so well, or so Anne had heard. Apparently he was prepared to tough it out. In an exercise in *extreme* self-control and professionalism, she'd told him that her door was open for him; so far, he hadn't knocked. She sincerely hoped he would. His first book had knocked the wind out of her like few others had. He did it once; she really felt he could do it again.

But there were other authors to consider, as well. There were other writers that could craft a story like Yates and Franklin and Goldman. It was too early to admit it yet, but—

Yes, she liked the feel of *Bestseller.* She wasn't into it enough to really give it the old *Siskel and Ebert* two thumbs up, but she was certainly going to give Gerald Morgan one more chance.

Besides . . . Randy Goldman had been crazy, too.

She placed the lipstick in the medicine cabinet where it wouldn't roll off the counter again, and left the bathroom.

She was suddenly struck with that instant knowing, that split-instant sensation before her body actually acknowledged the truth. It was the split-second fairy that came and whispered in your ear *'hey, you're about to get the shit scared out of you, so jump'.* She'd been looking at the floor as she strode into the kitchen, and the dark shadow at the door was unmistakable. The split-second fairy spoke, and she jumped and gasped even before her eyes reached the dark silhouette on the other side of the kitchen.

There was a man standing at the screen door.

twenty three

"Jesus, ma'am. I'm sorry. I really am."

He had been standing at the door for only a moment, his arm raised, his fist clenched, about to knock, when she came around the corner. She stopped, gasped, and her hands flew to her face.

And he felt horrible. *Horrible.*

Anne composed herself, allowing her hands to fall to her waist. She controlled her breathing, but her clanging heart was going to take a few minutes to slow down.

She placed one hand between her breasts and managed a smile.

"No, no. It's okay. You just . . . startled me, that's all."

"I am so sorry. *So* sorry. I didn't know—"

Anne raised her hand. He was sincere, and he'd apologize all day if he had the chance.

"It was nothing," she reiterated. She flashed another smile, a genuine smile, and the man smiled back.

"I'm Cliff Stevenson." He pointed. "From over 'cross the lake."

Anne had already moved to the door and she opened it, inviting him in. "Anne—"

"—Harper," the man finished for her. "George told me all about you. Just as pretty as he says."

Anne blushed faintly and rolled her eyes. "Thank you. I'll have to give George a bigger tip this year."

Cliff laughed. Otto had been correct, as Stevenson appeared to be in his mid to late fifties. He had a rugged, stoic appearance. Gentle eyes. Fifteen years ago, Cliff Stevenson would have looked like a model for a cigarette ad—the ones where the guy wore a western duster and sported one of those fuzzy caterpillar mustaches—before the lung cancer ate away at his body like maggots. Now, Cliff Stevenson could have been the guy down the block that was always tinkering with the mower, the guy that always waved and said hello. The guy that played ball and flew paper airplanes in the yard with his grandchildren.

Except, of course, that he lived in the middle of nowhere.

"Don't want to bother you," he explained, "but I'm heading in to Three Corners. Can I bring you anything back?"

"No, thanks," Anne replied. "I've got to make some calls this evening, so I'll be going there myself."

Stevenson glanced around the room, his eyes bouncing from one manuscript to another. "Any good ones?"

Anne turned, glanced at the piles of submissions, and turned back again. Stevenson spoke before she could reply.

"Otto told me. You're an agent. You come here every year to read. George says you're pretty famous. Know a lot of important people."

Anne smiled again. She couldn't help but like the guy. He was honest and forward. Her type of person. "Well, I don't know about that," was all she said.

"You know Tom Clancy?" he asked.

"Well, yes. No. I mean, yes, I've *met* him. Once. I don't represent him, though."

"Fine writer. That *Red October* book was great."

Anne agreed that it was.

"Wilbur Smith?"

Anne laughed. "Sorry," she said. "Never met him."

"Great writer."

"Yes. Yes he is."

She and Cliff stood in the door discussing books for ten minutes. Finally, he said goodbye, and insisted that if she need anything, *anything,* to just come over, anytime, day or night. Doors are always unlocked. A thin trail wound around the water's edge all the way over to his home, and he gestured in its direction. *There are some soggy spots, so don't wear your good shoes,* he'd warned, pointing to his own muddied boots. She told him thank you, and that, if she needed anything, she would take him up on his offer. Cliff Stevenson left and disappeared into the forest.

twenty four

The only time he had really panicked was when she walked into the bathroom. She was a mere three feet from *him—three measly feet*—and if he'd even *breathed* she might well have heard it.

And when she spoke out loud—well, he thought he was going to have an orgasm right then and there.

How had she said it? Oh yes: *Okay, Morgan . . . stop it. Your story is freaking me out.* Even now, as he stood in the confines of the water heater cabinet, he felt as if his balls were going to explode.

Okay, Morgan . . . stop it. Your story is freaking me out.

She was enjoying it. He *knew* it. He had even—God forbid—thought about calling the whole thing off. He could walk away, right now. After all, this was what he had wanted in the first place, wasn't it? Someone who wanted his story, someone who would sell his story to the big guns?

No. Too fucking late for that. Way, *way* too late for that. A few years ago? Maybe. But now, there were too many other details he'd have to take care of. Details that he would have needed to take care of *before* he'd even traveled here. No, it would be too difficult to ditch the plan now and try and reach for the glory. Besides . . . he hadn't *planned* it that way. It wasn't what he *wanted* anymore. His satisfaction would come from reaching for his knife and slitting the bitch's throat, watching her bleed, seeing the searing pain in her eyes. Oh, the sweet, sweet horror of it all.

Of course, that would come *after* everything else. There were many more scenes, many more paragraphs and details that would come before the final, glorious conclusion. Just thinking about it gave him a hard-on that he couldn't have beat down with a baseball bat.

He remained in the closet, listening to Anne and the man in conversation. The speech was muffled, but he made out a few things. Something about Clancy. And George Otto. Shit. That had been unexpected. He hadn't planned on whacking the old guy, but Otto had surprised him. Had no choice. He had been caught red-handed, inside the cabin. Now that he'd been spotted, he couldn't just leave him. He was a witness, someone who would be able to place him at the murder scene of Anne Harper.

When Otto surprised him by coming through the cabin door, the stalker had faked a panic, saying that he needed a phone or a radio. Needed to call home. It was just enough to throw the old man off guard. He smashed him over the head with one of the iron fireplace pokers. He barely had time to clean up the blood, stuff his body into a canvas bag, and haul the corpse into the forest before Anne arrived. That had been a bit too close.

From his hiding place in the bathroom, he also heard Anne say that she would be going to Three Corners later that evening, which was *splendid.* Not only would it give him the opportunity to slip out of the small room without being noticed, but it would also give him the time he needed to set a few things up.

His patience returned. *Yes, I can wait, Anne. I can wait all night, right here if I have to. I'll do it for you, Annie.*

And then, lo and behold . . . the man left, and Anne sat down at the table. She picked up *Bestseller,* and began reading.

twenty five

She read *Bestseller* for a while, then read a few other submissions. Nothing drew her interest. Perhaps, she admitted, *perhaps* it was because she was so intrigued by Morgan's piece. Maybe she was interested in *Bestseller* simply because of the way and manner it had been presented to her.

She pushed the other manuscripts aside, adding two more to the *no* pile, and one to the *long shot maybe if you do a lot of rewrites* pile. *Bestseller* remained open to chapter seven, and she sat down and picked up the page. As she read, she circled the sentences and paragraphs that seem to parallel with her current surroundings. She read for a while, paused, then glanced out the dining room window to see the

ghostly, shimmering aura of the trees reflecting on the surface of the water.

Moments later, she again raised her head and saw the

shiny green hummingbirds were hovering at the feeder like little winged cigar stubs.

Cripes. It's like he's been here.

Some of what she read was far too descriptive and unnecessary. He'd spend an entire page describing a sunset, when a single sentence would have sufficed. Yet, in other places, Morgan was succinct and to the point.

But it was the story itself that was interesting. The plot was tight, the story moved at a good pace, and Anne found herself increasingly engrossed, not without a tinge of—

Fear?

No. Not fear. Fear was when she'd read *The Amityville Horror* when she was twelve. She read the book cover-to-cover in one evening, while her parents and brother were away at a Cub Scout awards banquet. *That* was fear, by gosh. Sure, *The Amityville Horror* was just a book, sure it was make-believe (even a twelve year old can separate bullshit from baked beans). But the story was *good.* It was *believable.* She'd scared herself silly reading that book, and had a hard time even getting up from the bed for fear of seeing glowing red pig's eyes glaring at her, or small ceramic lions at the bottom of the stairs waiting to bite her leg. When her family had returned home, they found a shivering little girl on the couch, wrapped in a blanket to her eyeballs. Every single light in the house had been turned on.

No, *Bestseller* didn't inspire *fear,* so to speak, as much as it invoked *suspense.* Anticipation. She found herself wondering what was going to happen to poor Beth Huston, how she was going to get away. And the stalker in the woods. God, what a twisted character. Sneaking around, following her, getting into the cabin when she wasn't there. Going through Huston's drawers and

perusing her panties, lovingly fingering the fine fabric. One particular pair he held to his cheek, caressing his face with the soft, silky material. Over and over, across his lips, flicking his tongue out and tasting the dryness of the delicate cloth. Slowly, gently, down his neck....

Gerald Morgan knew that the story would attract her attention. The genre, the woman-in-trouble scenario, the psychological anxiety and tension—all heightened by the fact that the story, the way it was written, could be taking place right around her. He'd created it that way to grab her interest, to give it that extra flair. Writers were always trying to do something unique to get the attention of an agent or publisher. Morgan's approach was certainly all that, and more. It was different . . . and damned if it wasn't *good.*

Gerald Morgan, for gosh sakes. She shook her head. *Wait until I tell Candace.*

She stopped at chapter ten and looked at her watch. Six o'clock. Marta and Allie would still be at the movies. She had time for a walk before she would set out for Three Corners.

twenty six

When he was certain she was gone, he slipped out from the cramped space behind the hot water heater, closing the wood panel door and emerging into the modest bathroom.

He peered cautiously out the window to make sure there was no sign of her. He then peeked his head out into the hall and looked out the dining room window. Slowly, silently, he crept down the hall, stretching his neck, looking out the kitchen window.

No Anne.

He strode to the door, intending to slip out quickly and quietly. At the last moment he turned and saw the piles of manuscripts on the floor. *Bestseller* was on the table.

This will just take a sec.

He quickly strode to the table and smiled. Chapter ten. She was *moving.* That would mean things were about to get real interesting, real quick, for Anne Harper.

He knelt down and looked through several of the manuscripts. She seemed to have them arranged in some order, but that was of no importance to him. He flipped through a few of them, and read the names of their respective authors.

Steve Germain? Never heard of him. Charlene Allen? The *Charlene Allen, the romance novelist? Give me a fucking break. Mark Franklin? She actually brought* that *trash with her?* He picked up the manuscript, leafed through it, and smiled. *Of course,* he thought. *She'd need something to start a fire in the fireplace.*

Most of the other names he didn't recognize. Some writers had submitted entire manuscripts, others had sent only the first few chapters. He read some of their cover letters, some of their story outlines.

And he *smiled.*

Nothing he found could compare to what she was reading right now. No other manuscript was going to even come *close.* All of the submissions from would-be authors and wanna-be writers that she'd brought with her were just that: wishful thinkers. He knew that once she bit into *Bestseller,* the hook would be set. All he had to do was watch her get reeled in, like a trout on a line. Soon, Gerald Morgan would be more famous than any of these penny ante writers could ever hope to be. The name Gerald Morgan would go down in literary history.

For altogether *different* reasons, of course. But that was the point.

He returned the submissions to their proper places and crept to the door. He opened it slowly, paused only for an instant, then slipped outside and into the woods.

twenty seven

It was like walking through a zoo, only better.

Anne counted three deer, two bald eagles, several hawks, and dozens of other birds that she didn't know the names of. She'd even spotted a raccoon at the water's edge, chasing something in the shallows. It was real-life *Discovery Channel* and *National Geographic Explorer* all rolled into one, in super-wide screen with Dolby Surround-Sound.

And the colors. Deluxe-digital Technicolor. Everything was so lush and green. Flowers radiated dozens of glowing colors from milky whites and stop-sign reds, to sunset oranges and banana-bright yellows. Hummingbirds—she'd never seen so many—stole from flower to flower, their long needle-like beaks extracting the sweet juices hidden inside the blooming plants. She'd counted over forty of the finger-sized birds before she lost track.

She returned to the cabin. Seven o'clock. She'd read for a little while, then drive to Three Corners to pick up some groceries, call Candace for messages, then call home.

Thirty minutes later, she placed the last page of chapter ten face down on the table.

Jesus, she thought. *What's he going to do to her?*

Chapter ten was disturbing. The main character, Beth Huston, had no idea that a deranged psychopath was stalking her. She was taking it easy, relaxing in some faraway cabin, completely unaware that she was being stalked. Anne felt herself wanting to scream at her. *Look behind the tree! Look behind the tree!* Or *don't go there!* But as the reader, Anne was privy to information that the main character didn't have access to, and Morgan wove the plot, storyline, and characters like a finely-wrapped french braid.

And the stalker was a psychopath by every meaning of the word. He was motivated by hatred, by a tidal wave of fury. He wanted to kill Beth Huston not for money, lust or power (although the two latter principles *did* play a small role) but for *revenge.* Somehow, the stalker had been wronged by either Huston or the industry, possibly both. It wasn't clear just yet. Perhaps some other motives were involved, especially since the stalker was toying with her. And the things that he described doing to her. No, there was definitely *more* motive there than simple revenge. Had to be.

But it wasn't necessary for Morgan to have written the book to parallel her own current surroundings and conditions; the work was good, and the story could easily take place at any remote cabin on any small lake in any part of the country. In the world, for that matter. Morgan hadn't so much as mentioned Michigan's upper peninsula, but the fact that he detailed the area so well was proof that he was familiar with the area and environment.

And the part about the hummingbirds. God, that was just a warped ploy to horrify Beth Huston. In *Bestseller,* the stalker had

poured hydrochloric acid into the hummingbird feeder. The whirring birds, unable to smell the poison, would take one sip and drop instantly. By afternoon, the ground beneath the feeder would be littered with dozens of shiny green hummingbirds. Dead hummingbirds, and—

Anne looked at the hummingbird feeder hanging from the cedar branch. Two of the small birds hovered around the plastic cannister like busy fairies, sipping the clear sugar water. One buzzed off and two more came out of nowhere. They, too, sipped quickly, then zipped off into the forest.

She looked at the manuscript. She was drawn to the next chapter, desperately wanting to find out what Huston would do when she discovered the dead birds.

I mean, that's just sick. That's just . . .

She looked at her watch. Seven-thirty. *Bestseller* could wait. For Allie.

twenty eight

The road seemed bumpier on the way out than it did on the way in. The fact that she'd have to travel the road *twice* this evening wasn't something she was looking forward to. She was going to make certain that she got whatever she'd need at the General Store, so she wouldn't have to repeat the journey tomorrow.

Who am I kidding? she thought. *Of course I'll make the journey tomorrow. Just to call. Just to say hello. To say 'I love you'. To hear her laugh.*

At eight o'clock precisely, the silver-and-mud BMW pulled into the small store that served as a gas station, convenience store, and *'your headquarters for deer processing,'* as the sign out front read. Another sign proudly advertised that the store was an authorized distributor of *DEER KO-KANE,* a product that promised, according to the sign in the window, to *lead those giant monster bucks right to your blind!* The ad displayed a cartoon deer with tree-trunk antlers and a crazed, *gotta have more* look in its eyes. Jay Leno would have a field day with this one. Anne shook her head, wondering if they served the product in little silver spoons, or did the hunter just leave little rolled-up hundred-dollar bills all over the forest.

A pay phone hung on the wall just inside the door. Phone calls first, then, groceries.

She called Candace at home. No urgent messages, no *gotta come back to the office right away's.* Of course, Candace wouldn't have told her such a message if there was one. *No, I'm sorry,* she would have said to any callers. *Ms. Harper will not be available until next week. Yes, I understand. Yes, I know who you are. Yes, I know who you're with. No, she still cannot take your call.*

God bless Candace.

There were several calls from potential clients, though. Writers.

"Which ones?"

"Steve Germain," Candace replied in her heavy South African accent. "And Charlene Allen. Says she's got a few revised pages."

Sorry Charlene. It'll take more than a few revised pages. It'll take an—

"And *Mr.* Harper called."

Silence. Then—

"What does *he* want?" Annoyed.

"Same as always. Wants you to look at his manuscript. Says he's 'adjusted' it since last year."

"Fat chance. Did you tell him where I was?"

"He guessed. I didn't tell him when you would be back, exactly. Oh . . . and he wants to see Allison over the Labor Day weekend."

Dickhead.

"Fat chance of that, too." She shook her head. He had a lot of nerve. No brains . . . but a shitload of nerve.

When she and Chad were married, Anne had sold a nonfiction book that her husband had written, a kind of 'do-it-yourself-lawyer' book. It wasn't her field or genre, but . . . he was her *husband.*

The book floundered. Chad then wrote another one. A *better* one, he'd said. Then in 1998 came the now infamous baby-sitter incident when Anne returned early one evening to find him giving a rather salacious tip to the sixteen year-old daughter of one of his colleagues. Then came the divorce, the nasty headlines, all the messy garbage. Incredibly, Chad still pursued her as an agent, wanting her to present his work to a publisher.

Come on, Anne, he'd told her over the phone last year. *We're adults here. What's done is done. This is business.* He claimed he wasn't having much luck with other literary agencies.

That's because you burned all of your bridges, you idiot. Everybody knows you're an asshole.

Candace spoke again. "And a call from Dr. Gardner."

Anne suddenly felt like Wile E. Coyote at the bottom of the canyon, the part when the roadrunner kicks the anvil off the cliff and it drops a hundred feet and pounds the doomed animal into the ground. There's a simple puff of smoke, a cartoon sound of something hitting something hard.

But the coyote always survived. The coyote would be back after *these short messages, folks!*

Cartoons never got cancer.

Tom Gardner was Allison's physician. He'd been through it all, saw the suffering, the pain, the torment. He was, for all purposes, a father to Allie. Certainly more of a father than shithead had ever been.

"Did he leave a number?"

"Yes. Home and work."

It wasn't good news, Anne knew. When Dr. Gardner gave his *home* number, well, something was up. Something was *wrong.*

Shit. God damn it. God damn you, *God. You and what you've done to my baby. You should burn in hell for what you've done. You're one helluva shitty God and you do shitty things and . . . .*

No—wait. Stop, rewind. I didn't mean that. Really. I'm sorry. I'm—

"Got a pen?" Candace was all business, even at her home, even after-hours. Anne jotted the numbers down.

"Candace?"

"Yes?"

"Can you call someone for me?"

"Certainly." No hesitation. "Who?"

"Gerald Morgan."

There was silence on the line. The roadrunner dropped another anvil, and the coyote popped up from the crater with pinwheel eyes and stars circling his head.

"Pardon?" Candace couldn't hide her disbelief.

"Gerald Morgan. Damn, Candace. I know this sounds crazy, but he's got a pretty hot piece."

Skeptical laughter. "Morgan? *Gerald* Morgan? *Trash-the-office* Gerald Morgan?"

"That's the one. But wait, Candace. He wrote an apology. I'll let you read it when I get back to the office. Apparently there was some medical or mental condition that caused him to act the way he did. He got help, or so he says. He hasn't called you, has he?"

"Morgan? No."

"Call him tomorrow morning and tell him I'm very interested. Thank him for sending the manuscript. Nothing more. I'll call him when I return to New York. And . . . don't take any shit from him. If he's not sincere or genuine—like I *think* he will be—just hang up on him. He's not worth it to me or you. But . . . but I think he's changed. He's *really* changed. Wait till you read this story. Call him?"

"You got it," Candace chirped. "Anything else?"

"You're a gem, Candace. I'm all set."

"Take care, Anne."

Dr. Gardner was not at the hospital, or at his house. She left messages at both places, and whispered an apologetic prayer while she dialed home.

I'm sorry, God. I'm sorry about that shit I said earlier. I didn't mean any of it. I hope you—

Her thought was cut short by a thick, Latino voice. Spaghetti-sauce thick. "Harper residence. This is Marta."

Home.

"Hi Marta."

"Oh, Annie! How *are* you?"

There were the usual quick exchanges, the *everything is fine here's,* the *everything is going great's.*

"Has Dr. Gardner called?" Anne asked.

"Dr. Gardner? No. He has not called."

She could hear Allie talking in the background, pleading. *Is that Mommy? Can I talk to Mommy?* Anne could see her daughter reaching upward, her hands opening and closing like little flowers.

The phone clunked. There was a pause, a breath. Then:

"Mommy? Can I have a puppy?" No *'how are you'* or *'I miss you'*. Just—*Allie.* Plain and simple. Anne's smile spread like a fanned flame.

That's my baby.

"What kind of puppy?"

"A brown one," Allie piped. "A cute one. I've already picked his name."

"You have, huh?" Anne could see her daughter's blonde hair bobbing as she spoke, her tiny hands gripping the telephone.

"Wagsworth. Wagsworth A. Harper. I'm gonna call him Waggy for short."

"What's the 'A' stand for?"

"Allie!" Giggles. Eight-year-old *happy* giggles.

There was more. Lots more, and Anne listened to it all, listened to Allie's sweet voice raise and lower, grow and fade. Listened to Allie give her the entire plot and funny parts of the movie she had seen with Marta.

I'm sorry, God. I'm—

"Know what, Mommy? Me an' Aunt Mimi caught a toad today!"

—sorry.

She and Allie talked for thirty minutes. Allie, as usual, did most of the talking . . . and that was just *fine.*

"Baby, Mommy's gotta go now. Can I talk to Aunt Mimi again? Talk to you soon, okay?"

"Mommy! Wait! You have to sing to me!"

"Okay. But you have to sing with me."

"You start!"

The song was hokey, campy, and silly. Anne had made it up when Allie was in the hospital. When she'd brought Allison the alligator Beanie Baby.

Anne put the phone close to her lips. *"Little Allie-Gator, don't you bite my toes . . . cause then I'll have to reach out and bop you in the nose; Little Allie-Gator sittin' in the stream; time to go to beddy-bye and—"*

"—have a sweet, sweet dream!" Allison piped, finishing the last line for her.

"Goodnight, sweetie."

"I love you, Mommy."

"I love you, too, Allie."

Milk. Orange juice. Fat-free yogurt. Jelly, cold-cuts, a six-pack of one-calorie *Dr. Pepper,* some canned goods, and a bag of watermelon *Jolly Ranchers,* the sin of all sins. While standing in the checkout lane she had picked up the current issue of *Cosmopolitan,* but had placed it back in the rack at the last moment.

Why in the hell would I need more reading material?

twenty nine

Things always work out the way they're supposed to. Everything happens for a reason. When God closes a window, he opens a door.

Bullshit. Hogwash, superstitious *bullshit.*

He'd *planned* it this way. There wasn't anything remotely cosmic about it. Things were going his way because he'd *planned* them to go his way. This was *his* world, and *he* was God. He knew where she was in the book, knew what chapter she was at.

Oh, Anne. This is going to be perfect. Better than perfect, if there could be such a thing. And of course there is *such a thing, Anne. Because I am God. I'm* your *God, and soon, you'll do whatever I say. Thy will be done, Annie. Thy will be done.*

He had watched her climb into the BMW and drive off. She was headed into Three Corners at seven-thirty. He estimated that she wouldn't be returning to the cabin until eight-thirty at the earliest. He'd have well over an hour; all he needed was five minutes.

The sun had slipped below the trees on the other side of the lake. Dusk waited in the shadows.

Two minutes after the BMW left, the stalker emerged from the forest in a leaf-pattern cotton/polyester hunting suit, looking part paramilitary militiaman, part bank robber. Even his ski mask and gloves were mottled green and brown. Hotter than hell, but damn near *invisible* in the forest. In one hand he carried the knife; in the other . . . .

Hydrochloric acid.

He went to the feeder in front of the window and popped the lid open. Slowly, carefully, he

poured hydrochloric acid into the hummingbird feeder. The whirring birds, unable to smell the poison, would take one sip and drop instantly. By afternoon, the ground beneath the feeder would be littered with dozens of shiny green hummingbirds. Dead hummingbirds, and—

the little green shits wouldn't know what the fuck hit them. By this time tomorrow, there would be a mountain of dead hummingbirds on the ground. By no means was it a showstopper. Hell, no. But certainly a pants-shitter. She'd shit her pants over this one.

Why, Anne . . . I'm just getting started. I haven't even warmed up yet. And wait 'till you see what I do for an encore.

He emptied the jar of acid in the feeder and carefully replaced the lid. He walked back around the south side of the cabin, contemplating, wondering how much more of *Bestseller* she would read tomorrow. Or tonight. Would she read tonight? He'd have to be prepared if she did. Things were going to move a lot faster now, a lot quicker. His mind raced.

He whisked the screen door open and stepped inside. *Bestseller* sat on the dining room table, however, he didn't go to it. Instead, he paced. He looked around the cabin for a long time, thinking, plotting. He left quickly without disturbing anything in the cabin, and slipped outside.

Yes, quicker. Things are gonna kick into gear real soon. It's all coming together. It's all—

Headlights. Headlights were coming. He could hear the car now, jostling over potholes and ruts.

Welcome home, Anne. Get lots of rest. Tomorrow's a BIG day for you. For US.

He darted around to the far side of the cabin and vanished into the dark forest.

thirty

The car stopped and the engine faded. He watched Anne step out, pop the trunk, and carry two bags of groceries into the house. Night had fallen, and the forest crowding the cabin was dark. Spaces between cedar trees became gloomy caverns.

And the porch light didn't work. He watched Anne stand in the doorway and throw the switch a few times, but to no avail.

Tsk, Tsk. Now, how could that have happened? He smiled. He'd thought of *everything.*

Anne walked back to the car, retrieved the last bag of groceries from the trunk, and returned to the cabin. He remained motionless, watching her. He had work to do, but he couldn't help himself. This was so fun, so exciting. It was such a rush. The sneaking around, the cat-and-mouse and hide-and-seek game he was playing. He relished these activities, relished setting things up for the big finale. Coupled with the fact that Anne Harper was so goddamned *lovely*. What a treat it would be to see her naked body below his, pleading and begging.

And *bleeding*.

The kitchen window glowed yellow. He watched her put the groceries away. Again, like last night, his boldness grew. He had the advantage of the dark, even more so when she had lights on inside the cabin. He knew she wouldn't be able to see beyond the screens or windows with the glare of the interior lights.

He watched her move to the front door. She hesitated, as if peering out into the darkness. Looking . . . .

What's this? She's closing the door? No big deal. He just hadn't expected it.

Getting spooked, Annie?

There was a clunk as the door closed, and an audible *ka-klink* as the door locked.

Oh, Annie, Annie, Annie. Do you feel safer now?

He crept closer, only a few feet from the kitchen window, listening. Then he crept alongside the cabin, around to the front. After a few minutes he heard the shower suddenly burst to life, and he peered in the big dining room window and saw the bathroom door swing part-way closed.

Quickly, quietly, he stalked the shadows back to the door. He crept to the porch and bent down.

Okay, right . . . here . . . or maybe—

—here. His fingers found the key beneath the rock. He stood up, unlocked the door, replaced the key, and carefully returned the stone to its position.

Don't worry, Anne. This isn't in the book. This is just for me, and me alone. You think you can keep me out with a simple lock on the front door? Please, Annie. You're smarter than that.

The door swung open silently, and he entered the cabin. The shower was running, and he could hear the sounds of her shuffling about within the glass stall.

He walked down the hall and peered through the open bathroom door. Steam had already fogged the mirror.

Moving slowly, he tip-toed to the door and grasped the knob. He didn't turn it, didn't move the door one inch. He just wanted to be *there.* To be so close, so very, very close.

He released the knob and reached into the bathroom, index finger extended toward the misted mirror. His finger stopped less than an inch from the steamy glass.

Maybe a note for her? Maybe something catchy and clever? Perhaps something like 'READ ANY GOOD BOOKS LATELY?'

He drew back. It was unnecessary, unplanned. It wasn't needed. It would mess things up, and put things into play far too soon. Besides . . . it wasn't in the book.

The water suddenly shut off, and the shower choked out its last gasps. The stalker turned swiftly and walked to the front door, the rubber soles of his shoes moving soundlessly over the wood floor. He turned the knob, slowly closed the door behind him, and became the darkness.

thirty one

Dr. Pepper? *Check.* Pretzels? *Yep.* Napkin? *Two of them.* Allie-Gator?

The small stuffed Beanie Baby stood at his post, guarding the nightstand with his bulging eyes and over-sized teeth.

Anne lay in bed, sheet pulled up over her breasts. *Bestseller* lay on the bed next to her, and she held a dozen of its pages in her hand.

"Okay, Gerald. Where are we going?" She reached over and grasped her Dr. Pepper. Already the can had started to sweat, and she wipe'd the cold perspiration off with her hand. She took a sip, then set the can back onto the nightstand next to the stuffed alligator.

"None for you, bucko," she warned the creature. "You've gotta drive."

Two hours later. **Chapter Fifteen.**

Good God.

The story was driving her mad, for several reasons. First, some of the writing was just aimless rambling. Not an awful lot, and not a big problem, as she'd been able to wind-surf over most of it. An editor—Andrea Ryder, perhaps, she was *excellent*—would be able to take care of tightening up some of the loose spots.

But, more importantly, the suspense, the twists in the plot—*shit.* He'd been so close, so many times. He could have killed Beth Huston anytime he wanted. But he doesn't. He won't. He wants to watch her—

Bleed. Jesus, did he ever. The stalker in the story was beyond sick. He was downright psychotic.

Was the story far-fetched? Possibly. Maybe not. But Morgan was doing a really good job at keeping the intensity flowing. He was—

Screw it, Anne, she thought. *This is brilliant. Nutcase or not, Gerald Morgan has a bestseller on his hands. A genuine—*

She smiled, shook her head. *Bestseller.* It fit. It fit *perfectly.* There would be no more contemplation over this one, no sir. She was going to drive back into town tomorrow, have Candace prepare a contract, and get it over to Morgan in White Plains. Sent by courier. He'd have it by the end of the day. She couldn't wait to hear the tone in Candace's voice.

Gerald? Gerald Morgan? You're signing Gerald Morgan? THE *Gerald Morgan?*

Anne picked up the pages she had read, then looked at the clock. Two-thirty in the morning.

Nope. The rest will have to wait.

She fingered the pages, the chapters that she'd read while in bed. Morgan sure knew how to create a psychopath. That bit about the dead loon

hanging from the branch, a string wrapped around its neck in a crude noose. The dead bird swung gently in the breeze, and the stalker had tied a note to its leg. It read: 'Don't look now, Beth, but your GOOSE is about to be COOKED!' The sight of the dead creature made her

recoil as the images came to mind. That had been a tough part to read, but damn . . . it had been *effective.* The way he'd lead the main character through varying tensions and anticipations, and then the image of the dead loon, swaying gently to and fro, to and fro—

Enough, she thought, shaking the image from her mind. *Enough for one night.* She was tired, but excited. *Bestseller* was going to do well. She'd have no trouble closing a deal with this one. She'd already chosen the first few publishers she'd submit it to, and one in particular that she *knew* would snap it up like a dime on the street. Hell, faster than that.

Publishers were in the business of finding good pieces, the shit that would *sell.*

"Good night, Allie-Gator," she said to the lifeless creature on the nightstand. She clicked off the light, and a thousand crickets took center stage. They sang her to sleep.

thirty two

She'd read even more than he thought she would.

He watched her from behind the thick spruce, and had even ventured to within inches of the screen. He was so close he could almost read the text himself. He could read the chapter headers, oh yes. They were done in bold-face, and he could see them easily.

Here I am, Anne. Recognize this face? You've seen me before. Oh. I'm sorry. How can you recognize me behind this mask?

Ever so slowly, he reached both hands up and peeled away the camouflage ski mask. His eyes never left her profile, and he watched her lips move in pantomime as she read *Bestseller* silently to herself. Occasionally, she would bring a hand to her lips and gasp, or mutter something that he couldn't hear. He liked that. Impact. Impact is *good.*

Here I am, Anne. No masks, no hiding. His face was mere inches from the screen, shrouded by the night. *Look at me Anne. Turn this way. If you turn your head right now, there's no way I could hide. You'd see me. Go ahead, Annie. What are you waiting for?*

It was a dangerous thrill, yes, but . . . it *was* in the book. She just hadn't read that far ahead yet.

But she would.

What do they call it, Anne? A case of life imitating art? Or is it the other way around?

The stalker had work to do. Anne was already at chapter fifteen, a quarter of the way through the story. There were a few things he needed to set up, things that needed to be put into play.

But he found it hard to remove his gaze from her. The linen sheet had fallen below her breasts, exposing her soft, beautiful nipples. He couldn't take his eyes from them. Her breasts rose and lowered gently with every breath she took. He was *mesmerized.* His lust grew with every heartbeat and he felt himself becoming aroused, erect and hard. He could literally leap through the screen, right now, and she'd have no chance. In two seconds he could be upon her; three seconds he could be inside her. In four seconds he could be pumping away madly, in and out, in and out, in and out. And there would be nothing she could do. *Go ahead, Annie . . . scream. Scream all you want. Save some of it, though. You'll need it.*

In and out, in and out, in and—

From beyond the screen, he watched her. Watched her read, watched her lips. Watched the subtle rising and falling of her breasts.

God, Annie. You are so . . . fuckable.

But not yet.

Soon.

Slowly, slowly, he backed around to the far side of the spruce. The creatures of the night were his cover: whirring crickets, screeching bats, the single honk of an occasional nighthawk. All worked together to hide footsteps and movements. A moment later, the bedroom light clicked off. Anne was calling it a night.

And his was just beginning.

thirty three

Morning came, and brought with it a dreary, gray mist. The fog beyond her bedroom window was so thick that it swallowed up the trees. She could only make out hazy, dark forms of trees and branches. Black, white, and gray, like an Ansel Adams backdrop.

Anne got up, slipped into a pair of sweatpants and a large white T-shirt with Tigger emblazoned on the front, bouncing on his tail. On the back, it read 'TEE-AYE DOUBLE GUH-ERR'. She yawned, stretched. Walked into the living room, bare feet padding the worn wood floor. Gazed out the window.

The fog was so thick that the lake was nonexistent. Even the dock had disappeared, eaten alive by the giant gray curtain.

She looked at the stack of manuscripts on the floor. There were still a number of them that she hadn't read, and she'd go through those today. It was hard to believe that half the week was nearly over; she'd be returning to New York in just three days. Then, of course, it would take another day just to recover from the exhausting drive. Flying would have been easier. There was a commercial airport in Escanaba, only a two-hour drive from the cabin, but she had never flown here. The drive gave her time to think. She liked to see the countryside as it changed, liked to watch the noise and clutter and bullshit of New York City fade into quaint towns along the Hudson. North through the Catskill Mountains, which were beautiful any time of year, past Albany, through Syracuse and Buffalo, west through Canada to Port Huron, then needling straight up Michigan's I-75 into the upper peninsula. Sure, she probably could have found any one of a thousand getaway cabins within hours from where she lived—but that was the problem. It was too easy to go home, too tempting to run back to the office for something. A pen. A marker. Check messages. Check e-mail. Return a call here and there—

But not from here.

Here, in such a remote area, she was *gone.*

Going home, of course, would be the opposite. The beautiful wooded terrain would slowly yield to civilization, to cars and high-rises and horns and smog. Oh well. The drive was long, but you saw things that you wouldn't see from 30,000 feet above the ground. And with all of the new restrictions and security at the airports, well . . . an extended drive wasn't all that bad.

Anne boiled water for tea and selected the cinnamon-almond blend, a *dreamy mixture of nature's finest fruits, specially blended for an enchanting aroma and a rich, satisfying taste!*

She rolled her eyes. Whatever.

She sat at the table for a moment, both hands around the steaming mug, sipping the hot liquid. The grayness of the morning was pleasantly still. Even the birds seemed to be sleeping in, opting to wait until the thick mantle of fog burned off.

When her tea was empty she went to the bedroom, changed into a pair of jeans and a thin sweater, and walked to the door. She was going down to the dock. She slipped into one sandal, then, deciding to go barefoot, kicked it off.

The grass was wet and spongy, the dew crisp and cool on her skin. Her feet were quickly soaked above her ankles. The dock and the rowboat appeared in the gray gloom, fading into view like ghostly apparitions. She stepped onto the wooden planks and walked slowly, casually, looking down into the water. Leaned over the side of the dock. The water was a mirror, perfectly smooth and untarnished. Her glossy reflection gazed up at her.

Farther along the dock. The fog was so thick that even the trees that surrounded the lake weren't visible. Everything looked surreal, mystical. Across the lake, the flat sheet of water was devoured by the misty ghost.

At the end of the dock she looked up into the gray. She looked around. She looked—

Down.

In the water.

Light flashed in her head. A pounding began somewhere. Eyes widened, and her lungs tightened. Her face flushed with white-heat. Somewhere deep inside, a siren screamed. Glass shattered.

"Oh shit," she gasped, placing one hand to her mouth. *"Oh shit."*

thirty four

A dead duck, a mallard, floated in the water, most of its body beneath the surface. The animal had a fishing line wrapped around its neck, its feet, beneath its wing, and around its body. A black and silver cigar-shaped lure was hooked beneath one wing. The duck's beak was open, threaded by several wraps of monofilament. A single glossy, black eye stared blankly up at her. The bird had become entangled in the mess of line, and drowned.

Or—

Anne spun, looked back at the cabin through the haze, then looked back down at the dead creature in the water.

Enough was enough. This is too much of a coincidence. Isn't it? *Isn't it?*

She found herself talking to him as she walked back to shore. "That's enough, Gerald! You're going way, too far."

She stopped at the shore and looked around, then looked back at the end of the dock. On one hand, she felt a bit silly. On the other—

What is going on here? What is he trying to do? Or . . . is he trying to do anything? Is it just—

She walked back to the cabin, put on her shoes, and picked up her car keys.

From the pay phone at the General Store, Anne called Candace's cell phone. It was seven-fifteen; in Three Corners, the General Store was just opening. In New York, Candace was on her way to work, stuck in the morning rush. She could hear the snarled traffic before Candace even spoke.

"Find Gerald Morgan," Anne stated firmly, not responding to Candace's cheery greeting.

"Find him? Like, in person?" Candace was puzzled.

"Yes. Find him. Speak to him over the phone, find out where he is. I want to know where he is."

"Well, it's funny you should mention that. He called last night."

Anne paused and caught her breath. "He *what?*"

"He called last night. I called him right after I hung up with you. Left a message for him. When I called the office just this morning to check for messages, there was another message on the machine from Dr. Gardner, and one from Morgan."

Shit. Dr. Gardner again. Something's up.

"What did Morgan say?" Anne's voice was tense.

"Couldn't tell. I could make out the beginning when he said who he was, but the sound was really bad, like he was on one of those cheap phones. Lots of static and loud. Why, what's up, Anne?"

"Did it sound like a cell phone?"

"Mmmm, no. Sounded like a land line."

Anne hung up and called her office. At this hour, no one would be there yet. When the machine picked up, she punched in the two-digit access code. Instantly, the machine clicked, the outgoing greeting stopped playing, and a series of beeps trilled in her ear. They stopped. Dr. Gardner's recorded voice came on the line. "Annie? Tom. It's Tuesday, around nine p.m. Sorry we keep missing one another. Call me between five and six Wednesday evening if you can. At home."

Beeeeeeep . . . .

Then: Gerald Morgan's voice. Candace was right. The message was garbled and unclear. She could make out something about a manuscript, something about returning Candace's call.

If anyone had been watching, they would have seen Anne's countenance visibly change from night to day. A surge of relief poured from her like a spring runoff. She hung up the phone.

He returned Candace's call. He was home. He was in White Plains. Which meant . . .

It was silly. The whole thing. It was that damned book that had made her paranoid. Of course it was. Morgan had written a brilliant story, but wouldn't pull off a stunt that would require him traveling all the way to Michigan's upper peninsula, watching her every move, just to get her attention to create even more of an impact along with his manuscript. It would have been completely unnecessary, and a waste of time.

But now another fear nagged her. She couldn't think it, *wouldn't* think it. All she could do was try to fend it off. And waiting until five to call Dr. Gardner? That was going to drive her bonkers.

The Monster. The Beast. Cancer. It came back. Why else would he try and reach her when he knew she was in Michigan?

She picked up the phone and called his office. He was out of town, not expected back at the clinic until Thursday. She hung up, then dialed his home number. His three young sons took turns saying *sorry, but nobody's home (giggling) but leave a message (more giggling) and we'll call ya back soon! (laughter) Beep—*

Annie left a message saying that she'd call back at five, like he'd requested. She hung up the phone, climbed into the BMW, and headed back to the cabin.

thirty five

Improvise.

He hadn't planned on her leaving like she had. He thought he'd have a bit more time. Five more minutes, that's all he would have needed. Five more minutes, and Anne wouldn't have gone to town. She wouldn't have been able to. He had, however, gotten a smile when he heard her shout at him.

Annie, Annie, Annie. Right by the book . . . or close enough.

But he hadn't expected her to go to town. That surprised him. Oh, he knew she'd be back. She'd left everything there. Her clothing, manuscripts, toiletries. Everything. She'd be back. Soon.

And that changed a few things. He'd already had to leap ahead a little and try to guess what her next move would be. He'd been busy most of the night, and had allowed himself only a few hours' sleep.

And the duck. Jesus. He'd almost fucked that one up. *Badly*. His intention was to hang the duck at the end of the dock, not leave it floating in the water. But while he was making preparations, he heard the beeping of the microwave. He was on the goddamned dock and she was in the kitchen! Through the fog, it was difficult to make out where she was Hell, he could hardly see the cabin. He'd barely been able to slip back up the dock and behind the shed before she sat down at the dining room table.

Now, he'd have to switch a few things around. He'd have to skip a few things, jump ahead a little bit. That was okay. It just meant that he couldn't screw around anymore. He'd have to dump a few chapters and move the story along.

He glanced at his watch, calculating the maximum amount of time he would have. He was conservative about it: he knew she'd be going to Three Corners, probably to use the phone. She'd gone shopping last night, so it was doubtful that she'd be spending any time in the General Store.

There was, of course, an entirely different problem. What if she really had suspected something? What then?

Then everything would be off. It would be a shame, but if the plug had to be pulled right now, it wouldn't matter. He could walk away without worries.

No. The duck had freaked her out. She'd found it too soon. But she doesn't suspect anything. It's the book. The book is what is freaking her out. She knows it. I know it. It's the book.

He glanced at his watch again, then stepped out from behind the shed, crossed the yard, slipped into the forest, and continued through the thick brush. There were several places around the cabin that he used as hiding spots; any one of them would do fine right now.

He stepped behind a large spruce and waited for Anne to return.

thirty six

She sang to the radio. Matchbox Twenty said *If you're gone, baby, you need to come home.* She liked that one. And if a song came on she didn't know, she hummed along. Then she popped in an audio book. Daniel Silva's *The Kill Artist.* Awesome. The audio book took her mind off the monster, the 'C' word, the rest of the way back to the cabin. She knew that once she got there, she could immerse herself in manuscripts for the rest of the afternoon. Until four-thirty, at least. Until she would make the journey back to Three Corners to call Dr. Gardner.

By the time she returned to the cabin, the fog had still not lifted. The air was chilly, and she nuked a cup of water and opened the box of Bigelow samplers. The only flavor left was

Almond Chamomile. She'd had it before; it sounded like the name of a lizard, and tasted like it, too. She settled instead for instant coffee.

After moving the entire pile of *haven't got to these yets* to her bedroom, along with the blue scrapbook, she crawled onto the bed. She flipped quickly through the pictures of Allie, allowing herself only a few quick glances and smiles. No sense getting emotional now. She didn't know what she'd be dealing with in

Six hours and twenty minutes from now. I can get through the rest of these submissions.

Anne placed the scrapbook on the floor.

"Okay, Allie-Gator," she breathed. "Time to get down to business."

Hours later. A dozen manuscripts later. She'd gone through the rest of them, the entire *haven't got to these yet* pile. Nothing exceptional, but she'd pushed several off to the side to put in the *better have another look* pile, and she marked a few to go in the *hey-this-isn't-bads.* Jeremy Seeger's *For These Eyes* was moved to the *I think this is pretty good stuff* pile, along with Gerald Morgan's *Bestseller,* which she'd purposefully stayed away from. She already knew she wanted *that* book. She'd finish reading that one tomorrow, or perhaps when she returned to her office.

All the while, she kept an anxious eye on the time. The minutes seemed to move pathetically slow; glaciers were faster than her watch.

At four twenty-five, she got up and transferred all of the manuscripts to their respective places in the living room and around the fireplace. She'd managed to keep the 'C' word contained under lock and key, thanks to her diligent reading efforts. She'd even fanned a spark of optimism, telling herself that Dr. Gardner just needed some records. Yes, that was it. But—

Call me at home, Anne. Call me at home.

She didn't like the sound of that.

She tidied up the cabin, gave everything a once-over dusting, then grabbed her purse, and left for Three Corners. She'd been so busy around the cabin that she hadn't even noticed the growing number of hummingbirds on the ground beneath the feeder.

thirty seven

At four fifty-three, Anne pulled into the parking lot of the Three Corners General Store. At four fifty-five, she held the pay phone in one hand, dialing with the other.

The phone picked up on the first ring.

"Hi Tom. Anne Harper."

"Annie! I'm glad we finally hooked up." His voice was cheery. That was good.

"Sorry I've missed your calls. I've been out of town."

"So I've heard. Hey. I've got some results back."

Anne held her breath, keeping down the balloon that was billowing in her chest. She didn't need to ask him further. Tom Gardner told it straight, no flowers and honey, no pussy-footing around. He was compassionate, but he was direct.

"It's back, Anne."

The balloon exploded, and Anne felt dizzy and hot. Her skin crawled. Fear gnawed. She fought back, holding it in.

"How bad?"

"I think we can get it. I'm damned ninety-nine point nine percent sure, Anne, and I mean that. It's in her pancreas. It's serious stuff, I'll tell you that right off. You need to know that. But we found it early, Anne. In its earliest stages. I'm telling you . . . having Allie tested consistently paid off, Anne. In a few months it might have been too late. But *now* . . . ."

Her mind was reeling. A thousand thoughts flitted and dived around her like sparrows, and she grasped one as it swooped by. She closed her eyes. "What do . . . what do I need to do? Where—"

"She's in no immediate danger. She's not going to have any symptoms, she's not going to notice a thing. But I want her back here. *Now.* As soon as possible. We're booked for weeks, but Allison can't wait. We have a golden opportunity to take care of this before anything more serious develops. I want to get this taken care of *now.* Can you get her here day after tomorrow? Friday?"

"She'll be there tonight if you need her. I'll have Marta fly out with her, and I'll catch a flight from—"

Gardner laughed. It was a relaxed laugh, a soothing laugh, and it put her at ease. "Anne . . . take it easy. It's early in the game. Don't misunderstand me—this is serious. But we've got a *big* lead this time. Not like last year. I'm telling you—and this is *me* talking—Allie is going to be *fine.* See you both Friday. Friday at three, my office."

Me talking. Code for *no bullshit, Anne. This is it, on the plate. Like what you see? Too bad . . . we're going to handle it together. This is* me *talking.*

"See you Friday. And Tom—"

"—thank me when you get here, Annie. Friday."

She smiled. "Friday."

Anne terminated the connection by placing her hand on the telephone receptacle, then let it back up. She could cry later. A dial tone buzzed, and she called Candace. There were things that needed to get done. She'd be leaving today, this very evening. That would put her back in New York by morning. That would—

"Anne Harper Agency, this is Candace."

"Candace—Annie. Allie and I need a flight to Minnesota Friday morning. Rochester." Pleasantries were not disbursed. She gave Candace the specifics, but didn't go into details about Allie. "Just some more tests," was all she said. "I'll be leaving here—" she glanced at her watch— "in an hour and a half. I've got to go back to the cabin and pack. I'll be in the office by morning."

"That's a long haul, all night like that."

"I have to, Candy. I *have* to." Long, heavy sigh. "I'll wrap up whatever needs to be done at the office, then go home. I'll be gone for the weekend. Maybe longer."

"Give me another call just before you leave tonight, so I can be here when *you* get here. I'll come in and get the coffee started."

"That would be great."

"Anything else?"

"No." She paused. Then: "Wait."

"Yes?"

"Thank you, Candace. Thank you for everything you do." She didn't cap the sentence with an *'I really mean it'* or *'just wanted you to know that.'* What she'd said was enough; anything else would have been church clothes.

"No problem, Annie. Drive safe."

"Okay, *Mom.*"

The short stint of laughter was strained, but it was good. Candace had a pretty good idea what was going on, and it was a stiletto to her *own* heart. Even when Gardner had called a few days ago, she knew something was up. *Again.* She'd gone to church that night, lit a candle. Thinking about what Allie, and a lot of other children, had gone through. Talking to Anne this evening had left her soul bleeding. She was sure that if she looked beneath her desk she'd find the carpet sopping and stained with blood. That's what the monster does to you. Cancer. It was a goddamn beast, conjured from the novels of H. P. Lovecraft or Edgar Rice Burroughs. Her sister had died of cancer five years ago; Candace couldn't imagine one of her own children stricken with the disease.

Quick goodbyes. Anne hung up with Candace, then called home. The phone rang and rang.

Shit. It's Wednesday. She looked at her watch. *Swimming lessons. Marta would have taken Allie to swimming lessons.*

She hung up the phone, walked back to the BMW, and headed back to the cabin to pack. She was going home. Back to New York.

Then to Rochester, Minnesota. To Mayo.

Sometimes the monster comes out of nowhere, Anne, Gardner had told her last year. *There are no reasons. He just shows up. There's nothing you could have done differently.*

Now she *did* cry. She pounded the steering wheel, the seat. She cursed God, then apologized. Cursed him again. Nothing helped.

thirty eight

Three mistakes. That's all he'd made so far.

Almost getting caught beneath the rowboat had been one. The noise in the water heater closet was next, although that worked out fine.

And not getting the duck in place in time this morning. Anne was supposed to see the duck, jump in the car, take off, and—well—get a special surprise. He'd miss-guessed the time, and that didn't allow him to get the rest of the plan in place. Snagging a duck with a sinking Rapala fishing lure turned out to be no easy trick. A loon would've been better—that's the way it was written—but there weren't any loons in sight that morning, so he'd settled for a mallard. He'd hiked to the stream and threw some bread in the water.

A dozen ducks showed up to dine on the morsels. Tossed out the lure dozens of times. Each time a duck would go for the lure, thinking it was food, then turn away at the last minute. Finally, he'd landed the lure right behind a big female. He snapped the line hard and *whamo!* Duck ala spinning rod. The bird quacked bloody murder. Noisy little bitch. She tried to fly, tried to swim off. He'd reeled her in and snapped her skinny little neck with a stick, then wrapped a few feet of line around its body. Ducks get caught in fishing lines all the time. Maybe Anne would think it was an accident, maybe not.

And that was *exciting.*

To make her wonder, to make her worry. To watch her as she began to add things up and realize what, exactly, was going on. Damn. It was just like . . . *a book.*

While Anne was talking to Gardner on the phone in Three Corners, the stalker had been busy. It was *time.* Time to bring the reader to the shattering climax. He had spent only a few minutes in the cabin, as the props there would only be minor details. There were other, more . . . *involved* specifics that would require a bit of skill that had nothing to do with the cabin.

And she'd missed the fucking hummingbirds. I put a lot of work into that, you cunt. The least you could have done was appreciated the effort. A lot of little birds died today, and you couldn't even attend their funeral. Well, it makes sense. You're a literary agent whore. Why would you have a heart for something that wasn't making you money?

He'd screwed up his opportunity to get things in motion with the duck, and now the hummingbird holocaust was supposed to kick everything into gear. He'd waited for her to walk outside, or even see the tiny birds dropping like rocks. Then: Pow! Zap! Zowie! Things would really start happening.

But *nooooooo.* She was preoccupied in the bedroom, reading cheesy manuscripts by no-name wanna-bees.

And she wasn't even reading *Bestseller,* for chrissake.

Fucking cunt. Goddamn literary agent whore.

But, he thought, *it's no problem. No problem at all.* He could wait it out and adjust his plan. He was author, editor, and publisher. He could do whatever the hell he wanted. Even the delay hadn't been a problem. It just gave him a little more time to relax and plan. He'd waited patiently, waited for her to either take a walk or row out onto the lake.

And right now, he was going to get into position and wait.

He walked through the woods, waiting for Anne to return. It was largely ceremonial, and he didn't want to miss it. After all, it would be the last time that Anne returned to the cabin. Sure, she'd try to leave . . . but that wasn't an option. *It wasn't in the book.* He estimated that he'd have less than five minutes, if that. Probably less. When Anne walked into the cabin and saw his little surprises, she would turn right back around, hop in the car, and leave. No packing, no locking up the cabin, nothing. Christ . . . she wouldn't even take the time to grab that stupid toy that she talks to.

And, of course, she wouldn't be going, far, huh-uh. She wouldn't be going far at all.

He passed the split in the two driveways where one angled off to the cabin on the other side of the lake. Then he reached a small clearing. The two-track driveway cut a swath through a cluttered field, choked with waist high grass and weeds. Small wildflowers bloomed, and a few bees made their daily rounds, buzzing from flower to flower. He hunkered down into the thick weeds, glanced at his watch, and shifted in place to get more comfortable.

He stretched, shifted again.

And waited.

thirty nine

It had taken a lot of effort, she had searched and searched, and finally . . . she found it. Tucked neatly away in a little cupboard in her mind. She opened the door, and there it was:

The bright side.

She looked there. Gardner's words comforted her as she drove.

This is me talking. It's early in the game. We've got a big lead this time. Not like last year, Anne. This is me talking.

The car sped along the highway until she came to the old dirt road. After several miles of bumping along, she came to the two-track that, were it not for a red and white sign that said *Otto,* would have been nearly invisible in the dense forest.

She turned onto the weathered road and the car bounded along, crying out over every bump and pothole.

It's back, Anne.

She turned the radio volume up, but all she heard was Dr. Gardner.

And what would she say to Allie? She'd always been truthful, always been up front. They'd faced the leukemia together; they'd face this together.

But how would she explain it? Allison was eight years old. All of the memories would flood back to her. The pain, the needles, the chemotherapy. The lengthy hospital stays. What was Allie going to think?

Anne would have twelve hours to think about it.

Rounding a sharp turn, the forest fell away and opened up to a wide field. Then the trees returned and the two track crept along the side of a steep embankment. On her right, the passenger side, the hill sloped upward. To her left, the hill dropped sharply, and the view of the countryside was spectacular. Vistas of green trees and swelling hills. An endless, Scandinavian-blue sky. A few towering pines grew taller than their surrounding forests, and their spiny tops jutted majestically into the sky. Anne slowed, admiring the beauty of the evening. Then the road took another sharp turn and the forest swallowed up the BMW again. Sunlight flashed through the thick foliage like firecrackers.

The two-track opened up and the cabin came into view. The early evening sun burned high above, and the air was still and calm. She'd miss the place, but she didn't take the time to think about it.

She stepped out of the car and walked quickly to the cabin. Her mind whirred with things she'd have to get done. Pack, leave a note for George. She'd place the rest of the money she owed him in the microwave, like he'd requested his renters to do. Gas up the car at the General Store. If there was one thing she had to do between now and Friday, there were a million things.

She opened the screen, then pushed the door open. The screen door whisked shut behind her, banged on the frame.

She stepped inside . . . and froze.

All of the manuscripts were gone.

forty

The manuscripts should have been arranged in neat piles on the floor around the fireplace, the couch, the table. Like they had been when she left an hour ago.

Every single one of them was missing.

Except for . . . *one.*

Anne moved slow, dream-like. Her mouth was open in shock as she approached the table.

No. No, no, no. Can't be.

On the table, *Bestseller* sat, open to where she had left off last night. Beside it, a mug of tea waited. Almond chamomile, the lizard blend. She could smell it. A wisp of steam trailed up from the dark liquid. It was still warm. On the page where she'd left off, a note had been scribbled:

No fair reading ahead, Anne. Let's take it page by page, shall we? —GM

In the middle of the table sat an unopened bottle of wine. Merlot. The compressed air wine opener lay on the table next to the bottle. A note on a small piece of paper said

For when we're finished, Anne. When YOU'RE finished. When you reach THE END.

Her mind blurred. He *had* been here! Shit! Last night! He must have called his answering machine from here, in the upper peninsula. Checked messages. He returned Candace's call from somewhere up *here!* He'd been here all along, stalking her, watching her.

Waiting for her.

Her head snapped from window to window and she expected to see him, standing next to a tree or within the thick alders, watching her. Smiling. His scraggly beard untrimmed, hair wild. Bug eyes, blazing with crazed madness, fixated on her.

A hummingbird screeched to a hovering halt at the feeder, its wings a blur as it sipped the sugar water. Then, without warning, the bird fell. It was as if it were a wind up toy, and it had simply wound itself down. Anne leaned forward and looked at the ground beneath the feeder.

A carpet of shiny green hummingbirds lay dead. Their wings were folded and tucked in, and they looked like little green lipstick cases, all piled together en masse. Two or three were twitching, their fragile wings fluttering in short, rapid spasms.

Her horror mounted. *Oh, God. He's doing everything in the book. He's here. He's—*

She spun around and raced to the kitchen. There would be no packing. That could wait. Everything could wait. She had to get out of here. Now. *Hell, he could be here, in the cabin, right now!*

She threw open a kitchen drawer. Silverware clanged. She pushed aside forks, spoons, other items.

There. A knife. Sharp, with a long, silver blade. She snatched it up and whirled.

Swish, bang. She flung the screen door open and it slammed against the side of the cottage, then banged shut behind her. Anne ran to the car, knife in hand. Her eyes darted back and forth, expecting to see Gerald Morgan pop out of nowhere.

He'd been here. *Was* here. *Is* here. Shit. *Shit!*

She reached the car and leapt inside. Her heart drummed, and her breathing was quick and shallow. Time spiraled.

He was here! Is here! Jesus! He's crazy! She fumbled with the keys, and the engine roared to life.

The police. I'll go to the General Store. Call the police. Wait for them there.

Gravel spun as she whipped the BMW around. The car set off down the two-track, flying over potholes and bottoming out on ridges and bumps.

She was going to make it, and she allowed herself a hint of relief. She was in her car, she was on her way. She was safe.

He's lost it, she thought. *A long time ago. The cover letter was all bullshit. All of it. There was no 'medical condition' at all. Gerald Morgan is a madman.*

At the clearing the two-track smoothed a bit, and she pressed harder on the gas pedal. The car responded, sailing along the road. Grass and brush smacked at the sides of the car as it sped forward. The remaining cassettes of *The Kill Artist* bounced from the seat, scattering on the floor.

Suddenly, the car began to weave wildly. Anne grasped the wheel, fighting for control. The wheel felt loose, and the vehicle responded sluggishly, like it was on ice.

Like—

No! No!

The bumps in the road slammed the car harder than ever. Each time the tires hit a rough spot the car shuddered violently.

And then she *did* lose control. The car suddenly jerked sideways and careened into the field, jolting to an abrupt stop only a few feet from the two-track.

forty one

Anne leapt from the vehicle.

Holy shit. Oh, God.

The tires of the car were completely flat. Each tire had several steel balls—razor-jacks—buried into the rubber. Each ball had spikes protruding out at several angles, deadly sharp, designed to rip and tear and permanently damage car tires.

Anne looked around, searching the field. Her heart galloped. He was here. Somewhere. She knew he was. He was playing with her. It was his game, his—

Book.

Shit, Anne! her mind screamed at her. *How could you be so stupid?!?!* What she had thought to be a unique attempt to get her attention wasn't just a story. Jesus . . . it was real. Morgan wrote it with the intention of—

What? What was he going to do? How could I be so damned stupid?!?! He's been—

Stop it. Think. Think!

Her eyes continued to scour the forest. Everything looked so peaceful, so calm and serene. Unseen birds sang high in the trees, and insects whirred in the meadow.

But no Gerald Morgan. No—

The knife. Get the knife now.

She reached into the car and snapped up the steely blade. It wasn't much comfort, kind of the way the chair was to the lion tamer. Sure, it was *something*, but if that lion wanted your ass, he was going to get it.

Think.

She whirled again, peering through the trees, wondering if he was watching her this very instant.

Morgan's been at the cabin. He probably knows the woods. It's twenty miles to town. I could walk, but it'll still take me over an hour just to get to the highway. Morgan might have a car. Must have a car.

Where could she go? Back to the cabin? She could use the CB radio and call for help.

No. Morgan might be there. He might have been there when she returned, waiting for her. That's what he wanted, if he was going by what he'd written in his book.

What to do. What to do.

Or, more importantly . . . what did *he* expect her to do? The plot of *Bestseller* mimicked exactly what he was doing to her now, almost to the letter.

But she hadn't finished reading the story. She didn't know how it ended. She didn't know what poor Beth Huston would do . . . or if she even made it out alive.

She had to out-guess him. She had to do what he hadn't planned on her doing. *But what had he wanted? What does he want?*

The book on the table, the wine. The razor-jacks on the two-track. He wanted her to go back to the cottage. *That's* what he wanted. He *intended* her to go back to the cottage. That was what he expected, she was certain.

Never happen, you bastard.

Think. Where could she go? Who would—?

Cliff Stevenson. The other side of the lake. The tires had blown out just past the split in the two-tracks. One went to Otto's cabin, the other wound around to Stevenson's. She could follow the long driveway and be at his cottage in five minutes, tops.

forty two

Now the chapters were *moving*, and the story was racing to its climax. It wouldn't be long.

The razor-jacks had worked *perfectly*. After Anne's car sped by, returning from Three Corners, he had leapt out and scattered them across the two track, jumped back into the forest, and waited. She'd be coming back this way a lot sooner than she had expected.

Four minutes. In four minutes, he heard the BMW racing through the forest like a steel rhinoceros, engine revving, metal slapping twigs and branches. It whipped around a corner and came into view, and the stalker hunkered a little lower, keeping beneath the tall grass and brush. The car suddenly lost control, and he watched it grind to a sudden halt not twenty yards from where he was huddled.

She leapt from the vehicle, inspected the damage, retrieved something from the car, and set out. He watched her walk through the woods. She couldn't see him, but she sure as hell tried. He *knew* she was looking for him. She knew he was there, somewhere. He *knew* she knew. Her head bobbed around, searching like a kid on an easter-egg hunt.

And the knife she was carrying.

Ha. Good luck with that one, Annie. Paul Hogan's line in Crocodile Dundee drifted into his head. *'That's not a knife—THIS is a knife . . . .'*

Anne turned and began running down Stevenson's two-track, to his cabin.

This is going to be good. You're in for a real treat, Anne Harper.

He followed her at a distance, knowing that she'd be turning her head around every few seconds to see if he was behind her. He was like a deer hunter, waiting for the prime moment, that perfect window of opportunity for the kill. The stalker kept close to the trees, and when he saw her turn her head he froze, blending in with the mottled leaves and wiry branches of the surrounding forest.

You'll go to the old man's cabin, he thought. *Then to your cabin. Then you'll finish the book. Why? Because that's the way it's written. That was* why *it was written. Especially the end, Anne. You'll especially enjoy the end.*

He kept a safe distance behind her, watching her run, wondering what would go through her mind when she finally reached the cottage. He tried to visualize the scene in his mind, tried to visualize her terror.

And she deserved it. Oh yes, she did. She was a literary agent, Supreme God to all writers. He was doing writers all over the world a *favor,* for chrissake.

But, he admitted, he was doing it for *more* than that. He was doing it for the rush, for the sport of it. He'd done it before; this time was just so gloriously *intense,* so acute and mesmerizing. He'd been freebasing adrenaline for weeks, living on the high of the planning, the preparation, the *knowing* of what would happen. Every new idea, every new thought was like a blast of euphoria racing through his brain.

And it would be all over the headlines, all over the news. Someone would probably write a book about it. Someone would write a book, complete with *sixteen pages of shocking, never before seen photographs! The bizarre murder that shocked the literary world! The stunning New York Times—*

Bestseller.

Ahead of him, on the two track, Anne was racing toward Stevenson's cabin.

And he followed.

forty three

Halfway there.

Gerald Morgan was everywhere she looked. Her head snapped nervously around, and she swung the knife out in front of her. She saw him behind trees, hiding in branches, crouching behind rotted, moss-covered stumps. His bulging, crazy eyes peered out at her from the knotholes of trees. His wild, gale-swept hair wove through branches and limbs. He was in the pines, he was in the swamp, he was in the lake that flashed between the trees as she got closer to Stevenson's cabin. He was—

The cabin. There it is. Thank God.

Cliff Stevenson's cottage was partially obscured by cedars. Anne saw the corner of a window, part of a porch railing.

Please be home, Cliff. Please be home.

She ran faster, and the two-track widened and became a driveway, circling around the west side of the cabin and coming back around several small, rustic outbuildings. The trees fell away and she was in the open, running, running beneath a late evening blue sky, racing across the open grass, her feet pummeling the ground.

"Mr. Stevenson!?!?" she shouted, even before she had reached the home.

She glanced around nervously, expecting Morgan to come flying at her out of nowhere, his eyes swollen with insanity.

"Mr. Stevenson!!" She had reached the door, and now she pounded with her fist, hard, then leaned over and peered through the living room window. The cabin was laid out similar to Otto's except it was a bit more spacious. A log couch was backed up to a knotty pine wall, and above it hung a large fish with a red and white lure dangling out of its mouth. A very 1970-ish television set was tucked into the far corner, and several logs were stacked in a stone fireplace, unlit. A deer head was mounted on the wall. It glared back at her with glossy, dark-brown eyes.

"Mr. Stevenson!!" she shouted again. She tried the door.

Locked.

He said the doors are always unlocked! Always unlocked!

Again she glanced nervously around. She was in the open, vulnerable. The knife was a small comfort, but not much.

She stepped off the porch and ran around the cabin. Checked another door.

Locked. Checked the windows.

"Mr. Stevenson!!"

Locked.

She pounded the window with a flat palm.

"Mr. Stevenson!"

She looked over at the sheds, at the small outbuildings. One was simply a crude portico. Piles and piles of firewood were stacked beneath it.

And then:

Music. Anne heard a radio playing somewhere close by, coming from one of the small buildings. Country music. Alan Jackson's *Chatahoochee.*

Her eyes darted from building to building as she walked, trying to determine where the music was coming from.

Oh, thank God. Thank God.

There. In one of the sheds, the front of an old blue Chevrolet truck came into view. The hood was up, and a utility light hung over the engine.

"Mr. Stevenson?" Anne called out as she jogged toward the garage.

"Cliff?!?!"

She reached the garage. The door was partially closed and she pulled it open.

Had anyone been within a half-mile, they would have heard her scream. Had anyone been near, they would have stopped what they were doing and rushed to help.

But not today. Today, Anne's horrified shrieks were lost in the forest.

But the stalker heard her, and he smiled.

God, did he love that sound.

forty four

"Oh Jesus!! Oh God!!"

Anne dropped the knife, and it fell to the grass with a *chik* sound as the blade penetrated the soft ground, then fell on its side. Anne's hands flew to her mouth. She screamed, jumped back, and froze. Her breaths came in short spasms, *hu-hu-hu-hu-hu,* like a bicycle pump, and it was hard for her to exhale. She stared, her eyes transfixed by the sickening sight.

Cliff Stevenson's lifeless body hung from the rafters by a rope. A noose had been fashioned around his neck, and his arms dangled loosely at his sides. His eyes were swollen open, bloated and empty. They stared back at Anne, unseeing, unfeeling.

And the *note.*

A single, letter-sized piece of paper was pinned to his chest by a knife, of all things. The blade went through the middle of the paper, and a thick stream of blood had stained the note, his shirt, and his blue work pants. Below him, a dark stain of blood the size of a garbage can lid was seeping into the sand floor. The pool had already started to dry. The note read:

HOW'S THIS FOR A CLIFF HANGER, ANNE???

Oh God. Cliff—

Anne heard a noise and spun. At a birdfeeder near the house, two blue jays were scooping up seeds, chasing one another around the feeder, making a lot of noise in the process. She turned back around and faced Stevenson, then noticed the truck tires. Slashed. At least the two that she could see. She wouldn't be going anywhere with this vehicle.

Then she saw something else.

His pocket. There was another note in his pocket. She hadn't seen it before. It was smaller, folded, but even from where she stood she could read the word on the paper:

FOR ANNE.

For me? Why would Cliff have a note for me, unless—

Maybe he was going to warn her. Maybe he'd written the note to leave at her cabin in case she wasn't around. Maybe—

She was shaking as she took a step toward the lifeless body. She focused on the paper in his pocket, trying to avert Stevenson's pained, dead glare. Then, after taking another glance behind her to make sure Morgan wasn't coming at her, she reached out and yanked the note from the pocket. Her hands were trembling so badly that she dropped it. It fell, landing in the dark stain in the sand.

Still shaking with fear, she bent down and picked up the folded paper. She opened it up, instantly recognizing the ink-splattered letters.

The note was from Gerald Morgan.

Dear Anne:

By now, you've no doubt read quite a bit of Bestseller, and I'm hoping that you've found it to your liking. However, I've noticed that you aren't quite finished with it. I'll bet you're just dying to find out what happens to Beth Huston, aren't you, Anne? I'll bet the suspense is just killing you. Well? What are you waiting for? I've arranged everything you need for you to finish reading, Anne. Tea. Wine. It's waiting for you, right now. Oh . . . I've also arranged someone else to wait for you, Anne. She really wants to see you bad. Don't worry—no harm will come to your daughter, unless you don't play by the book.

He's lying. You goddamn bastard! You're lying! Tears ran down her cheeks, and she continued reading.

Oh, I know exactly what you're thinking, Anne. How could I possibly have your daughter? I can't, can I? Well, maybe I don't have her. But I know someone who does, Anne. He has her right now.

Adrenaline surged with the force of a gun. *You're a LIAR! You're a fucking LIAR!*

He's an awful, awful beast. He could do things to your daughter that would be far worse than even I could imagine. And he's ready, Anne. He's so ready. He's just waiting for the word from me. Your daughter is so pretty, so very lovely. I would hate to have anything happen to her, wouldn't you? Finish the book, Anne. Finish the story. Do it—for Allison.

"YOU'RE LYING!" she screamed at the letter, choking back sobs. Her voice rose through the forest, scattering the birds at the feeder. She spun, her eyes searching the dark shadows between the tree trunks. The forest was still. *"YOU'RE FUCKING LYING AND I KNOW IT, MORGAN! I* FUCKING *KNOW IT!!"* The tears came heavy now, and she couldn't catch her breath. Thoughts collided like freight trains.

He's . . . he's lying. He's lying. He's—

They weren't home this morning. Allie and Marta. No one was at home. No one answered the—

It's Wednesday. Swim lessons. Swim lessons.

He's an awful, awful beast.

She's with Marta. She's safe.

He could do things to your daughter that would be far worse than even I could imagine.

"WHY ARE YOU DOING THIS?!?!?" she screamed, sobbing. *"WHY? WHAT HAVE I EVER DONE TO YOU, YOU SICK BASTARD?!?!"* Her voice rose high, then was quickly muffled by the thick forest.

Why is he doing this? she thought. *And how?* It made no sense. *Why would he submit a manuscript, only to do this? What did he hope to gain?*

Nothing made sense. He was a lunatic, a madman. She had known it since the day he'd sent his first manuscript to her.

But she couldn't have known about *this.* Shit . . . how long had he been planning this? Where was he going with this? And Allie—

He's lying. Isn't he? He has to be. He's—

Going by the book! *The son of a bitch was going by the book!* In *Bestseller,* the stalker had threatened Beth Huston, saying that he'd kidnapped her daughter . . . but he *hadn't.* It had only been a ploy, just another one of his sick ways to torment her.

Gotta get outta here. Gotta get help. Police.

She turned and looked across the lake. The water shimmered blue and bright, an aluminum pancake beneath a cerulean sky. At the end of a graying old dock, Stevenson's rowboat bobbed in the water. A fishing pole was on the seat next to an oar. She turned around again and saw the front of the blue Chevy. It looked oddly hobbled with the wheels slashed, like an old, arthritic dog struggling to stand. She'd be going nowhere with *that.* Three Corners was too far away.

Hide. Hide somewhere.

Where?

Inside Stevenson's cabin. Break a window. Break a window and get inside.

She retrieved the knife from the ground, keeping her eyes focused on the silvery blade; nothing else. She couldn't bear to look at the hanging body one more time.

I'm so sorry, Cliff. I had no idea. None. I still don't.

But she knew one thing. In *Bestseller,* things weren't looking good at all for Beth Huston, New York literary agent extraordinaire.

Was that what this was all about? Morgan is pissed because I won't represent him? Would he really do something like this? And why would—

A movement. Out of the corner of her eye, something moved on the two-track. She flinched, turned—and froze.

It was *him.* Standing in the middle of the two-track, a hundred yards away. He was head to toe in camouflage clothing, holding a knife, just standing there, watching her.

And then he began walking toward her, his steps deliberate, purposeful, arrogant. After a few quick steps he began jogging, then running, his legs pumping like pistons, the knife swinging wildly at his side.

forty five

Anne sprang. Her heart slammed inside her chest like a mallet. There was no time to smash a window and get into Stevenson's cottage.

The radio! The radio at my cabin! I'll get inside, lock the doors and windows! I can radio for help!

She dashed through the yard and found the trail that wound along the lake. She needed to put as much distance between her and Morgan as possible. Her legs churned, and her shoes thumped the trail. Branches slapped at her face and arms like sharp, wiry tentacles.

Like Cliff Stevenson had warned, the trail was muddy and rugged. She leapt over pools of black, mushy goop. In other places, the mud was unavoidable. She trudged on through, her feet sinking over her ankles, making a maddening, *hwuuuk* sound with each frantic step. It was like running in pudding.

Every so often she managed a quick glance behind her. She saw no sign of Morgan, but she wasn't going to take the time to look for him. She knew he was coming.

Gotta get to the cabin. The radio. Lock the doors, get on the radio. Channel 9, the emergency channel. Her mind whirled. *But Morgan can still get inside. He can smash windows!*

And her car was out of the question. She might have tried it if only one tire was flat, but all of them had been destroyed by the razor-jacks, shredded like cheddar cheese. If she tried to drive, the car would be uncontrollable, especially on the uneven two-track.

I've got a knife. And the fireplace poker. There's two of those. I'll boil water. I can throw it at him if he tries to come inside. But—

What if he had a gun?

No. He doesn't have a gun. He doesn't have a gun because the killer in that damned book doesn't have one.

The cabin appeared through the trees. It seemed to dance among the trunks and foliage, and her heart rose. She would make it.

Yes. Almost there. Anne snapped her head around. She still didn't see Morgan, but the trees were thick. She was sure he wasn't far behind her.

Quickly, across the short yard. Up to the screen door. She ran up to it so fast that she slammed into it. She threw the screen open, then fumbled with the doorknob. Leapt inside. Behind her, the screen whisked and banged closed. Anne slammed the heavy door shut, securing the dead-bolt.

The radio. Get the radio.

She sprang to the fireplace mantle and snapped up the two-way.

Power. Where is the power button? There.

She pushed a small red button on the top of the unit and brought the microphone to her mouth, about to speak.

Wait a—

She pushed the power button again. Nothing happened. She hadn't used the radio since George Otto had shown her years ago, but she was sure she remembered the dial lighting up, the speaker crackling with static. She flipped it over and popped open the battery case.

Inside, four Energizer D cells were nestled together, two-by-two. All of them had puncture marks, like they had been stabbed with the pointed end of a knife. All were leaking greasy, brown-green acid. A tiny, hand-scribbled note taped to the back of the battery cover read:

Sorry Anne . . . these batteries are DEAD—
But I'll keep going and going and going . . .

The pit of devastation became a canyon.

Barricade the doors! Close the curtains!

She placed the radio on the counter and raced around the rooms, locking the windows, pulling the shades. The rooms grew darker, murkier, cavern-like. The couch was heavy, but she managed to push it against the door.

Water. Boil a pot of water and scald that bastard if he tries to come inside.

Her hands were shaking as she held the pot under the faucet. It seemed to take forever to fill it with water. When the water was just below the edge of the pot, she placed it on the stove and turned the gas burner to high. There was a faint hiss, and the flame ignited with a popping *whoosh.*

She retrieved the knife from the mantle and picked up a heavy iron fireplace poker. She gripped both weapons like they were her last hope in the world. Maybe they would be. *After all,* she thought with raging sarcasm, *even* I *don't know how my story ends. Even I—*

The manuscript. The book. *Bestseller.* It sat on the table where he'd placed it for her to read, along with the mug of tea, the bottle of wine, and the opener.

He *wanted* her to finish it.

He's following the story. He's patterned what he's doing to me after his story. He's doing the same things to me that he did to Beth Huston. Maybe—

She picked up the manuscript and took it with her to the hall, where she sat on the floor. From there, she would have a view of the bedroom window, the bathroom window, and the rest of the cabin. With the shades and curtains drawn she wouldn't be able to see outside. But Morgan couldn't see *in,* either. And if he tried to get in, she'd at least have a chance of defending herself with either the boiling water, the knife, or the poker. Then—

Shit.

It was dark in the cabin. When the sun set, it would be pitch black. She'd have to leave the lights off so Morgan wouldn't know exactly where she was . . . but she wouldn't be able to see, either.

She got up quietly, carrying the knife with her, and retrieved a candle from the kitchen drawer. She lit it from the open blue flame from the gas stove. Eerie shadows dipped as she walked back down the hall. She sat down, placed the candle on the floor, the knife in her lap.

She waited, listening. Every sound caused her to jump. She listened for footsteps outside, she listened for anything. Dozens of frantic thoughts raced through her mind.

The manuscript. I have to find out what he's doing.

She picked up the remaining chapters of *Bestseller,* and began reading where she had left off. She'd always prided herself on being a slow reader, a reader who savors each word like fine wine, sampling each and every delicious note. Now she read quickly, and her eyes raced from sentence to sentence. Her head nodded from side to side like she was watching a tennis game in fast-forward.

And she read.

forty six

It was even better than he'd imagined. Better than he'd planned, better than he'd written.

He'd watched from the two-track, hidden off to the side between two enormous pines. He could see her pounding on the door of Stevenson's cabin and calling out. He saw her run to the shed, saw her drop the knife, heard her scream. Watched her read the letter addressed to her. The garbage about her daughter was just that: *garbage.* That was just his way of fucking with her, like the killer had done to Beth Huston. *By the book, by the book.* He knew that Anne probably wouldn't believe it, but maybe she would. After all . . . she hadn't finished *Bestseller* yet. She had no idea what he was capable of doing.

But she would. Oh, yes. Would she ever.

And the old man? Expendable. How does the United States government put it during wartime? Oh yes. *Acceptable losses.* That was one. *Terminal non-existence* was another. It was a 'necessary' expense. And he'd made it work to his advantage. It wasn't even in the book, for crying out loud. Just something else to drive her insane and scare the shit out of her. But damn . . . that note stuck to his sternum was *clever.* That was a stroke of fucking genius; even Anne Harper, Literary Agent Queen that she was, could appreciate that. Originally, the note had said *'SEE? MY BOOK IS LEAVING EVERYONE HANGING'.* But when he saw the registration papers on the seat of the truck and found out his name was Cliff, well, that, my friends, was just *too* good. He couldn't miss that one.

Cliff-hanger. That was just fucking *brilliant.*

The longer letter had been planned, of course. The note to her, the bullshit about her kid. That one had taken a little bit of thought and preparation, and he tried to keep it word-for-word with the note in *Bestseller.* Of course, this meant that he'd had to do some re-writes to the manuscript, but that was okay. *Bestseller* had nothing to do with Beth Huston, for that matter. It had everything to do with *Anne Harper.* And the way it would all work out was *perfect.*

Now she had returned to her cabin. She was probably running all around inside, trying to find something to protect herself with. She'd close the curtains, lock the windows and door. Find the radio, and realize that she was fucked. Jim

Morrison and The Doors had said it perfectly thirty years ago. *Five to one, baby, one in five . . . no one here gets out alive.*

And she'll read. Sure she will. She'll want to find out what happens to poor, poor Beth Huston. And even after she finished the book, even after she figured it all out—

Well, by then it would be too late. Much, much too late.

He dreamed about the headlines that would be all over the papers.

Top literary agent tortured and killed; disgruntled writer suspected.

Ha. They were all in his hand. This time, *he* was calling the shots. He'd fool them all. He'd *screw* them all. The industry and everybody involved. What a shocker this would be.

And how did that Marine saying go?

Oh, yes.

Fuck 'em all . . . let God sort 'em out.

Or something like that.

forty seven

The sun dropped below the trees, and a thin strip of amber fire glowed in the western sky. Darkness cloaked the cottage, its enormous arms around the forest, suffocating the last fragments of daylight.

Inside the cabin, a tiny candle glowed. Every tiny creak she heard, any little snap at all—caused Anne to stop reading and glance at the windows. She was sure he wouldn't be able to see in and see the candle . . . not with the shades and curtains drawn, anyway. But even still, the tiny light wasn't any comfort.

And the book. Gerald Morgan's goddamned *Bestseller*. Concentrating had been difficult. She read in short, machine-gun bursts and then stopped, her head snapping around, eyes darting from window to window. As she read, the similarities screamed at her. Earlier in the week when she had read the synopsis and the first few chapters, it had been a clever way of getting her attention. The story had been just that—a story. Now she began to see how the plot had been written for her all along. And the more she read, the more obvious it became.

There were parts of the story that were, of course, slightly different than her own situation. But for the most part, the further she read, the more it looked like Beth Huston was in big trouble, mister. A *shitload* of trouble. Morgan was obviously following the plot of the book to the letter. Beth Huston was being tormented in the same ways Anne was.

She read faster and faster, trying to figure out what he had been thinking. What he *was* thinking, what he *was* planning. If she could figure out his next move, maybe she could outguess him. The only clues would be found within the manuscript itself.

Near the end of the book, during the last few chapters, everything changed.

Everything.

From the writing style to punctuation and spelling. There had been surprisingly few errors up until that point, but the last few chapters were *littered* with bad grammar; run-on sentences, unfinished paragraphs, paragraphs that had little or no meaning to the story.

And the *plot* changed.

No—it didn't just *change.* It did an entire one hundred eighty degree pivot. At one point Beth Huston had gained the upper hand, and it looked like she was going to escape. But suddenly, everything turned around. The final six chapters were nothing but pages of disgusting torture and rape and sadistic acts. It was written in the sense that the stalker had been the champion all along, that he was claiming some great victory for the world. After he had brutalized poor Beth Huston in ways that were simply beyond imagination, he had

slowly cut her throat with a razor and watched her bleed. It was wonderful. Awesome. Watching her eyes, watching her watch him come toward her with the knife. She was already dizzy from pain; the previous hour had been the longest in her life, he knew. Even so, she squirmed and wriggled as he began to slice her throat, left to right. Not too deep. The killer didn't want her to die suddenly, but rather, fade slowly into the dismal beyond. The blood sprayed like an erupting volcano, then trickled to a river. Beth made spastic, gurgling noises, sputtering like a badly-tuned tractor. Then, she stopped. Blood continued to trickle, only now it flowed in thin rivulets, like a fine merlot. The killer smiled and

The end of the book was a pathetically long paragraph, over three pages, glorifying Beth's murder, praising the stalker and how he had beaten the evil beasts of the publishing world by sacrificing their high priestess. Morgan had tried to write it like a western, where *our brave and courageous hero saddles his horse and rides off into the sunset.* If he'd been on medication the first fifty pages of the book, Anne could tell the exact moment that it had worn off.

Finishing the story left her shocked and drained. The book was beyond horrifying, especially now that Anne knew it had been written for her all along. Anne Harper *was* Beth Huston, the Main Character. The killer was the writer, Gerald Morgan. He had written the story to shock her, and hell . . . it worked.

Emotions boiled. Anger, fear, remorse. Impending doom and dread. *Why go this far? If he was angry with her for not accepting him as a client, then why not just kill her? Why go through the trouble to write a book, to do all the things that he was doing?*

And Cliff Stevenson. What had *he* done? Morgan had killed him just to get a reaction from Anne. He had watched her, saw her reaction when she'd discovered Cliff's lifeless body dangling from the rafters of the garage.

Night had crept in hours ago, without any sign of Gerald Morgan. With darkness came hope. If nothing else, she would have a better chance of slipping away at night. She blew out the candle, and the darkness welled up within the cabin.

She looked at her watch, and pressed the tiny button to illuminate the dial light. Midnight. The waiting was driving her mad. Why was he doing this? Was he still around? Or was he purposefully

waiting for the right moment. He wanted to let the terror sink in, to let her squirm and twitch and shake, so he left her in the cabin. She knew he was around, somewhere. He knew she knew. And for him, the waiting was delicious. He would wait until the right moment, and then he would

smash down the door. Was he planning to do the exact same thing that the killer in his story had done? In the story, Beth had escaped from the cabin, only to be caught in a

large field. He caught up to Beth and tackled her. She fought, kicking and screaming, but he had overpowered her.

Then, in a bizarre ritualistic fashion, he forced her to strip, placing all of her clothes in one neat pile. He lit them on fire, and laughed as the flames licked into the night. Beth tried to run again, but he tackled her. Only this time, he placed a dog collar around her neck, and clipped a leather leash to it. He ordered her to remain on all fours, and that, if she tried to stand up, he would plunge the knife directly into her anus. He placed the tip of

the blade between her legs, sliding the cold metal over the sensitive folds of her vagina. Beth froze instantly, choking back an earthquake of sobs.

"Yes, right here, Beth. You wouldn't like that, now, would you?"

No answer.

"Would you, Beth?" He gave the knife a gentle twitch and the tip of the blade entered her tender flesh. Beth jolted, her body taught and constricted. A tiny whimper came from her lips.

"Answer me, Beth. You wouldn't like that, would you? Because if you do, it could be arranged."

Beth choked out a few sputters. The word 'no' was coughed out in a half-whimper, half-wheeze. She shook her head.

"Good, Beth, good. I'm glad we understand each other. Communication is so important in a relationship, don't you think?"

He withdrew the knife. Beth was sobbing, choking uncontrollably, and he forced her to walk, on hands and knees.

"Good girl," he said, as if he were talking to a pet. "Good girl. We're going to have lots of fun together." He forced her to move this way, naked, crawling on the ground, all the way back to the cabin.

Anne shuddered. What the killer had done to Beth was unspeakable. Never, *ever,* had she read of such repulsive acts of brutal torture and violation. She wanted to run from the cabin, screaming, screaming for help, but there was nowhere to go. If Morgan was near, he could probably outrun her and track her down, like the killer had done to Beth Huston. And although the cabin was probably her safest place, she knew she was a sitting duck.

And we all know what Gerald Morgan does to ducks.

The water on the stove had boiled down. She got up quietly, slowly, and filled the pot again and placed it on the stove. That was something Beth Huston hadn't done. If Gerald Morgan was going to come in through the door—or a window for that matter—he was going to get showered with scalding water. She would make his skin blister into little bags of red jelly. He would scream like he made poor Beth Huston scream, like *he* wanted to make *her* scream. When Gerald Morgan came through the door, he was going to get a lava shower straight from hell.

She tip-toed back to the hall and sat back down. Waited.

And then, just before one a.m.—

Noise.

A rumbling. A car engine. Gravel. Headlights suddenly sprayed the cabin, and the curtains glowed. Anne's whole body tensed. She stood, grasping the knife with one hand and the fireplace poker with the other.

He's here. Jesus, God. He's here. He's here!

forty eight

She sprang to the kitchen window and peered out into the yard. The car had stopped, parking where she normally would have parked the BMW. The engine died. The headlights remained on, flooding the cabin. A car door closed.

Anne stood in the kitchen, watching Morgan. She placed the poker down and reached for the pot of boiling water.

Soft footsteps swished on dirt. A tiny twig snapped, a few small stones scrunched. Then:

"Anne?" a male voice called out.

She knew that voice. Yet—

"Anne? Are you here? It's me. Mark. Mark Franklin. Are you here? Are you okay?"

Franklin?!?!? Mark Franklin?!? The writer Mark Franklin?!? Oh God! Yes! Jesus, thank you! Oh Jesus!

How he had gotten here, how he had found her—none of that mattered right now. She unlocked the door and flung it open. She could see his silhouette in the car headlights.

"Mark! I'm here! Get inside! *Get inside!*"

Sensing her urgency, Franklin jogged to the front door, alarmed simply by her agitated pleas. Anne pushed the screen door open.

"What is it? What's going on?"

"Oh, God I'm glad you're here. She fell into his arms, and he held her. "Oh you have no idea! How did you—"

"Slow down, slow down." He withdrew from her, placing his hands on her shoulders. Confusion welled in his eyes. "What? What's going on?"

Anne closed the door behind him and bolted the lock. She flipped on the kitchen light. "Morgan! Gerald Morgan! He's here! He's—"

"What?!?! Are you sure?"

"Yes! Jesus! Oh, Mark! He killed Cliff! He—"

"Who's Cliff?!?!"

"He's—" Her mind spun. "Never mind. How did you—"

"Candace called me at home. She said Gerald Morgan called your office and threatened you. Said he was calling from some little town, some Corners—"

"Three Corners! Yes!"

"That's it. I passed it on the way here." He turned, thumbed the air. "I saw your car in the field back there. I saw the slashed-up tires, and I found metal studs all over the two-track. I kicked them to the side. Anne . . . what's—"

"But what did Morgan say? What did he say to Candace?"

"Something about if you don't accept his manuscript, he was going to do something."

"What?!?! *What?!?!*" She couldn't get information fast enough. She wanted to speed everything up, try and put everything together, already knowing that it wouldn't make sense anyway. None of it would. Morgan was a madman, plain and simple.

"She said that he didn't elaborate. Played it for the cops, but since he really didn't come out and say what he was going to do, they really couldn't do anything themselves. Since you have a restraining order, you can press charges. But that's about it. Candace called me because I'm only a couple hours' drive away. She just wanted you to be aware of Morgan. It was crazy trying to find this place! I got lost twice, otherwise I would have been—"

"God, Mark! You wouldn't believe what he's done! What he's doing! He's *here* Mark! He's *here!*"

"What?! *Where?!?*" He reached toward the kitchen window and pulled the curtain back, peering out into the night. The headlights lit up the yard, and monster-sized shadows lay poised in wait.

"He's been . . . shit. We have to get out of here. He's trying to kill me!"

"Gerald Morgan?" Mark spoke the words in disbelief. "Nutty Gerald?"

"We have to leave. Now! I'll explain on the way."

"Alright, alright. Calm down. You're fine. Let's get your stuff and—"

"No! She shook her head. "We have to go. Now! Find the police and—"

He placed his hands on her shoulders. "Anne! Take it easy! You're fine! Get hold of yourself. We'll go to the police. Just take it easy."

"What if he's out there?" Anne asked. They looked out the window.

"I didn't see anything on my way in. Come on. I'm here. You're fine. Everything will be fine."

"God, Mark! He wrote this story and—"

Mark raised his hand, silencing her. "Tell me in the car. Come on." He unbolted the front door and opened it a tiny crack, peering out into the night. Anne reached down and turned the gas stove off. Mark swung the door open. "Come on, Anne." He took her hand. "Let's go." The two stepped into the glowing headlights.

forty nine

Mark held her close, his arm around her shoulders as they walked quickly to the car. Anne's head snapped about, her eyes searching the dark shadows for signs of Morgan.

"I've never seen you this freaked out, Anne," Mark said as they reached the car. Anne quickly darted inside the Grand Prix and locked the door. She let out a sigh of relief and put her head in her hands. Franklin got inside, closed and locked the door. The car roared and began to move. Shadows ducked and darted, and the cabin disappeared as the car turned around and headed down the two-track.

"He's insane, Mark. He's sick. Like you wouldn't believe." She felt overwhelming relief now that she was safely in the car. "He wrote a story. It's about a lunatic that stalks and kills—no, stalks, *tortures* and kills—a literary agent just because she didn't accept his manuscript. He wrote it about *me,* Mark! He wrote it about me, and he tried to do all of the things to me that he did to the main character in his book!"

"Gerald Morgan? *The* Gerald Morgan?" Again, he expressed his disbelief. "I wouldn't think he'd be capable of plotting a trip to 7-Eleven, not to mention an actual storyline for a book."

Anne explained about the duck and the hummingbirds, about Cliff Stevenson, the note Morgan had written threatening her daughter. All the while Mark shook his head in between gasps of amazement.

"Today was a nightmare. *Is* a nightmare. He's been here all along. All week. Probably longer." She threw her head back on the seat and closed her eyes. "You have no idea how glad I am to see you."

Mark chuckled. "You have no idea how hard it was to find you. When you get away, you *get away.*"

"Never in a million years would I have thought that Gerald Morgan was capable of this. He's out of his mind."

The top of Anne's hobbled car came into view, hidden within the deep grass and brush. Anne shook her head. "I just can't believe . . . what have I ever done to him? I mean, sure, I had him arrested, but hell, Mark . . . he was tearing up the office."

"You got me. I can't believe that anything that wacko would do could possibly make sense."

"He's sent me manuscripts before. Awful ones. Terrible ones. And you know . . . the manuscript he sent me this time really *was* pretty good. The premise, the psychological intensity. His writing had really improved. Or, *I thought* it had, anyway. Up until the last few chapters. God . . . that was just *sick.*"

Mark laughed. "It's funny that he called it *Bestseller* when he's never had a single word published in his life."

"He's messed up, that's his problem. He's—"

The horror came slowly, seeping up through her socks, up her legs, her torso, her neck. Her head felt hot. She felt as if her hair was on fire. Mark's words burned in her head.

Bestseller. I never told him the name of the book. I never told him Morgan's book was called Bestseller.

fifty

Don't let him know. Don't let him know that I know. Keep talking.

"He's . . . shown a lot of improvement as a writer," she said, finishing her sentence. Her voice trembled, and she hoped he didn't catch it.

Don't let him know.

"He's a sick puppy, alright," Mark said, shaking his head.

It all made sense. She had wondered why Candace would have asked Mark to drive here, when she *knew* that Anne would be leaving to return to New York today. The thought had crossed her mind when he'd first told her, but her head had been spinning so fast that she had brushed it aside.

Think, Anne. Think.

What was his plan? What was he going to do? In his car, she was his prisoner. Where was he going to take her? What was he—

A field. Oh, God! That's what he's going to do! He's going to take me to a field and

placed a dog collar around her neck, and clipped a leather leash to it. He ordered her to remain on all fours, and that, if she tried to stand up....

She had to get out of the car. Quick. She had to get out somewhere and run. Someplace where he couldn't chase her with the car. Someplace where she'd be able to get a head start on him. But where? She couldn't wait. At any moment he could stop and pull out a knife. She had to get out. Get away. *Now.*

Where?!?! Where?!?!? Where would she go? No light, no knife. She had no weapon, no way of defending herself.

The ravine. It's coming up, right before—

The big, open field. There was a large field on the other side of the hill. That's where he would do it. He would stop the car and make her get out, force her to do what Beth Huston had been forced to do. Not because it was necessary, not because he'd chased her down . . . *but because that's the way it was written.* And she was sure, now that he had her, he was going to follow the book by the letter. The thought made her nearly vomit.

It'll have to be the ravine. The two-track winds around the side of the hill. The ravine is on my side. Steep. He can't follow with the car. When he slows around the turn I'll open the door. Jump. Probably fall down the hill. But he can't come after me with the car. If I can make it to the bottom of the ravine before he does, that'll give me a head start to—

to where?

Three Corners is out of the question. No other houses around for miles and miles. I'll have to hide somewhere. Somewhere. If I can just get away.

She could see the hill in the headlights, and the black emptiness of the gorge on her side of the car. Another thirty seconds.

It was him all along. It was Mark Franklin.

The hows and whys would have to wait.

It was him. It was him all along.

The hill suddenly loomed up to her left, and the ground beneath her door fell away into darkness. The headlight capped the tips of trees that grew along the slope. Then the trees vanished, and the lights spun into darkness.

Time's up, girl.

She knew that the ravine was steep: jagged rocks and trees grew up from the nearly vertical embankment, and there would be no clear path or even a solid foothold. And the valley descended for nearly a hundred feet or more. Her escape wouldn't be an easy one.

But it was the *only* one.

She waited until Mark had slowed the vehicle as it went around the turn. She placed her hand on the safety belt and covered it tightly, feeling the quiet *click* as it unsnapped. She held the belt across her lap so Mark wouldn't see that she'd released the latch. On the armrest, a small light glowed, indicating the door lock. Her fingers covered it, and her mind reviewed the plan in fast-forward, then rewind.

Hit the button, pull the handle, push the door, then roll. Hit the button, pull the handle, push the door, then roll . . .

Ready—

Anne took a breath. She fingered the door lock button.

Hit the button, pull the handle, push the door, then roll. Hit the button, pull the handle, push the door, then roll . . . .

Set—

Now.

fifty one

The door exploded open, the dome light lit up the interior. In one swift motion Anne threw the seatbelt strap away and dove into darkness. In a split-second, she was gone.

Franklin hit the brakes. Tires gnawed gravel. Red tail lights flashed. The car came to a sudden halt.

"Anne! Anne! What are you doing?!?!?"

She hit the ground at the very edge of the ravine, rolled, and tried to balance herself and get to her feet. Weeds ripped at her face. Her shoulder hit something hard, and she yelped in pain.

And then she was falling, plummeting in black vertigo. Her arms flailed madly in the darkness.

NO! I thought that—oh, God, no!

She had misjudged the steepness of the ravine. How much, she didn't know. But she was falling, straight down. In seconds, she would hit the ground, some hundred feet below her.

Wham! The unexpected impact struck her back with such force she was certain her spine had snapped. Breath exploded from her lungs. Hundreds of needles poked at her bare arms, her face, her hands. She'd hit a tree branch. It broke her fall and flung her sideways, and now she was falling again, needles splintering her skin. Her hands groped about frantically, grasping, trying desperately to grab onto something, to *anything* . . . .

The next tree branch caught her square between her legs. Blinding pain flashed. She gasped as her breath was forced from her with the force of a gun. The pain in her crotch was numbing. Her entire body went rigid, every single nerve aflame and white-hot. She lashed out wildly with her arms and grabbed the branch beneath her. She held it, feeling the sticky sap and the crinkled bark, but the blow to her pelvic region was too much, the pain too excruciating. She felt herself slipping, letting go—

No! No! Hang on! Gotta . . . hang . . . on.

Her body fell around the branch, but she managed to keep one arm looped over top. She dangled like a leaf.

Her feet touched ground. It was steep ground, and it plummeted down at a vicious angle, but it was *ground.* It was *solid.*

Above her, on the ridge, headlights glowed. She heard the car door open, heard the constant buzzing of the ignition warning. He'd be coming after her.

The pain in her lower extremities was subsiding, and she forced herself to gasp a breath. She had to move. She had to get to the bottom of the ravine. Where would she go from there? It didn't matter at this point. What mattered was that she needed to put some distance between herself and Franklin. Get a head start. She had a small one right now; she could lose it in a heartbeat.

She fell to her butt, still grasping the branch. Anne could see vague outlines of branches and a star-peppered sky, but there was no moon, and the night was deathly dark. She let go of the branch and began to slide.

"Anne!" She heard Mark Franklin shout from somewhere above. *"It's over, Anne! You can't get away. There's nowhere to go!"*

He said something else, but she couldn't tell what it was. She was sliding, trying to grasp anything that might slow her down. Rocks loosed and tumbled. Long blades of grass slipped and sliced through her hands like thin sandpaper knives. She succeeded in grasping a sapling, and it slowed her for a moment, almost bringing her to a complete stop before the roots gave way. She was off again, sapling in hand, sliding, tumbling. Her head smacked the side of a tree and she reached out to grab it, but it was too late. She rolled sideways and sharp rocks jabbed her ribs. Franklin was still shouting to her, but his voice was garbled like a badly-tuned radio.

Her body suddenly splashed to a violent halt. She hit solid, flat ground. Wet ground. Water. She opened her eyes. She was face up. Cold, shallow water—*freezing* water—rushed around her, in her ears, along her neck and sides. She was soaked.

The stream. I'm in a stream. The cold water jolted her senses, and she sat up. Her body ached all over. She was dizzy, and she shook her head. She stumbled when she stood up, fell to her knees, and got back up again.

"Annie!" Franklin called down to her. His voice was mocking and arrogant. *"I'm coming for you, Anne! Remember: that's how the story ends. That's how it goes, Annie! You were looking for another bestseller. Well, now you've got one! It's all yours, Anne! You've got your own fucking BESTSELLER!!"*

She looked up. High above, obscured by shadowy pines, she saw Mark's silhouette behind the car. The trunk was up, and he was digging around.

No more time, she thought. *Go. Go!*

Where? Upstream? Downstream? She had no idea where the stream came from, but, if it was like the dozens of other small tributaries that fed into Lost Lake, it probably fizzled out into nothing more than a series of small springs. Sure, she could follow it upstream, but that would just get her lost deeper in the woods.

Downstream? The creek fed into the lake, for sure. That would put her right back where she started. But at least she'd know where she was. Maybe she'd be able to find a place to hide. Stevenson's cabin. Maybe—

"Annie! There's nowhere to go, Anne!"

Stevenson's cabin. Cliff Stevenson was a fisherman. And a *hunter.* She'd seen the mounted deer head on the wall.

"ANNE!"

Hunters . . . *have guns.*

Anne fled, running through the shallow stream.

fifty two

Oh, she thinks she'll get away. That'll never happen. Sorry, Anne.

He heard the splash when she landed in the stream at the bottom of the gorge. She'd hit hard, he could tell. He paused, only for a moment. Maybe the fall had hurt her. Maybe she was unconscious. Then he heard splashing, footsteps. Branches cracking. She was moving. He returned his attention to the trunk.

She won't be going anywhere. She's not going anywhere I don't want her to go.

In the trunk he pulled out several items that he would need, one of which was a hand-held searchlight. One-point-five million candlepower. He could burn a hole in the moon with this baby.

He threw a large canvas bag over his shoulder—some special 'tools' he would be using—and slammed the trunk closed. Snatched the keys from the ignition, locked the car.

The scramble down the hill was difficult. He moved as quickly as he could, but he had to hold on to the light as well and keep the bag over his shoulder. Plus he had to use trees and branches to keep from falling. His feet slipped, and rocks tumbled down as they broke loose under his weight. If he lost his footing now, he would tumble down into the stream below. He almost fell several times, and twice the shouldered bag had slipped over his arm, causing him to stop his descent and swing it back into place.

He was angry with himself for not anticipating her escape. At what point had she figured it out? The bit about Candace calling? The razor-jacks? The—

Bestseller. I told her the name of the book before she told me what it was. I couldn't have known the title, unless—

It didn't matter now. Actually, this was an added thrill, a bonus. Even he didn't know how this chapter would pan out. It was like one of those idiotic *'create your own ending'* stories in which the reader, through a series of decisions, chose different endings to the story.

But he knew how *this* book would end. That's what counted. He knew how the evil villain met her demise. And she *was* the villain, that was for certain. He'd been a client of hers. Gave her a smash number one bestseller, he had. He was at the top of the charts for weeks and weeks. Yet she'd rejected every single one of his books since.

Sorry, Mark. This one just doesn't work for me. It's . . . it's different from your first one, Mark. Very different.

What she was saying was that it *sucked.* It sucked, and she didn't want anything to do with it.

He tried again. Worked his ass off.

I don't know what to say, Mark. You seem to be in a rut of some sort. I'm really sorry, but—

It sucked. He knew it. But there was a lot of other trash that somehow found its way to the publishing mill. Some of it was just a bunch of garbage. He was Mark Franklin. Bestselling author of *Theater of the Mine.* Why don't you accept *this* manuscript? His name alone would sell books, he had told her. Anne's reply had stopped him cold.

Mark, if the book you just submitted gets published as-is, even with heavy—and I mean heavy—editing, yes . . . it'll sell. But sales will fall, and soon, publishers aren't going to want to risk anything. Not even for you.

Besides . . . she was Anne Harper. Golden Girl of the Book World. She had a reputation to protect. Of course, these were Franklin's words, not hers. But he knew that if she started schlepping bad stuff to the big guns, they'd pay less and less attention to her. As it was, if Anne Harper approached a publisher with any manuscript that she was excited about, they'd be insane not to take it.

Which, of course, made her the literary agent that all the writers wanted. *Signed with Anne Harper? You're on your way to fame and fortune. Congratulations, boy, have a cigar. It's candy and roses from here on out.* He knew. He'd been there, done that, as that stupid saying goes.

Been there, done that. Couldn't do it again.

Well, in a way he *could.* He was doing it right *now,* as a matter of fact.

He reached the bottom of the hill. The lake glowed, silvery and shining in the moonlight. Mark swept the beam into the water. It reflected back up, bright, intense. She was following the stream back to the lake, and she would walk in the water so she wouldn't leave prints. He kept the beam low, sweeping it from either side of the stream and back again. She had a head start, but the light would give him an advantage traveling through the forest.

There. A track in the mud.

The footprint was faint and partially swallowed by water.

You're being careless, Anne. Remember, that's how Beth Huston slipped up. She was careless. And you are, too. It's only a matter of time, Annie. Just a matter of—

fifty three

—*time.*

And distance.

Time and distance. She needed both.

Her feet were numb from the cold water. Her whole body shivered. She'd fallen several times, stumbling over rocks or logs or branches. Once, she fell into a pool nearly two feet deep, plunging her entire body completely beneath the surface. The spill sent another freezing shockwave through her body. She sprang up instantly, wiping her eyes. Pressed on.

She had to outguess Franklin. *What was he planning now that she had changed the story? What would he do?*

Regardless, she knew exactly what would happen if she were caught. He would take her back to the cabin, whether he made her do it on her hands and knees or not. He would begin by

tying her to the bed, legs and arms apart.

"We have a long night together, Beth," the killer said softly. Beth began to scream, and he laughed. "Ah. I have just the thing," he said. In the dresser, he pulled out three of her socks and wadded them up. Beth closed her mouth instantly.

"Open wide," he said, in childish sing-song fashion. Beth shook her head, mouth closed, whimpering.

The killer drew a long knife from his bag and placed the tip if it to her vagina. He prodded her lips, ever so gently, with the blade.

"Wait!" she screamed, leaving her mouth hanging open like a hungry guppy.

"Much better, Beth," he said, pulling the knife away. He stuffed the wad of socks into her gaping mouth. "Now we can begin. First things first." He sat down next to her on the bed, holding the bag in his hands. "Are your ears pierced, Beth?"

Beth nodded. Whimpered again.

"There are several other places on the human body that people pierce. It's become very fashionable. Let's begin there, okay? Some new

piercings?" He reached into his bag and pulled out a large safety pin, holding it up for her to see. Beth moaned and struggled.

"This won't hurt a bit. I promise." Beth continued to struggle as he reached down and pinched her nipple between his thumb and forefinger. Beth whimpered, then choked a scream as the sharp point of the pin pierced her

The thought was revolting and she shoved it aside. Still, the visions of what had been done to Beth—the agonizing abuse, the sadistic torture, all of it—would not leave her alone. She'd seen it; she'd been there. In her head, she'd watched in stupefying horror as the killer did all those things to Huston. She tried to shake the images away, tried to erase them from her mind, but they kept creeping back. There are some things that you cannot un-see.

Anne stopped to catch her breath. She bent over, hands wrapped around her knees, gasping. She shivered.

He's a monster. A beast. He's—

Images of Allie suddenly flashed in her mind. In the hospital, at Mayo. Allie crying as a needle had been inserted in her arm. She saw her daughter in bed, wasted, dying, helpless, attacked by a—

Monster. Sometimes the monster comes out of nowhere, Anne. There are no reasons. He just shows up.

Behind her: a faint flicker. A light. She started off again, the horrible images of poor Beth Huston as the killer tied both hands and feet. The socks in her mouth made it difficult to breath. Tears rushed down her temples, around her ears. She was sweating, her body glistening, her muscles tense. The pins in her body felt hot. The killer just stood there, admiring his work. No movement, just . . . watching. She tried to speak, tried to talk, but the balled socks in her mouth gave her tongue no room to move.

The fire in the fireplace still burned brightly, and he walked to it and retrieved an iron poker that he had placed in the coals. The end of the poker glowed yellow-red with heat, and he brought it to the bedroom.

God no! What's he going to do?!?!? What is he—

The killer waved the hot poker over her body like a wand. She froze. Her eyes bulged, begging, pleading. He lowered the poker slowly, until she could feel the heat of it above her breasts. It remained there, all orange and glowing. She could smell the searing-hot metal, a caustic, chemical stench.

No! No . . . please! I'll do anything!

He loved watching her. Loved watching her wriggle and squirm, loved the way her eyes bulged like that of a stuffed animal.

He lowered the poker, down, down, lower, over her belly, lower. She could feel the heat on her skin. He waved it, waved it around like the poker was a

magic wand and he was going to stun the audience with another amazing trick. The glowing iron was now only inches above her dark pubic mound. She could smell the melting follicles, the stench of burning hair. Then, without warning, he

Enough! Anne's mind screamed. *Enough. No more. Stop thinking about it. Music. I'll think about music. I'll think about—*

It was funny, but the only tune that would come to her was the silly alligator song that she'd made up for her daughter. The tune drifted into her head and she hummed lightly, concentrating, focusing . . . .

Little Allie-Gator, don't you bite my toes—

The stream widened, and she was nearly running now, splashing.

Cause then I'll have to reach out and bop you in the nose—

The stream widened further, and the thick trees fell away. Thousands of stars appeared.

Little Allie-Gator, sittin' in the stream—

The creek deepened to her waist. She pushed through until it grew shallower. Stumbled, almost fell. Ahead of her, the stream opened wide, wider. No longer a stream at all. She turned and climbed out.

Time to go to beddy-bye and have a sweet, sweet dream.

She had made it to the lake.

fifty four

Through the trees, she could see the glowing lights of her cabin. To the west, on the other side of the lake, blackness. Stevenson's cabin had been swallowed up by the night.

Hunters have guns. Hunters have guns.

She turned and began to walk, arms outstretched, trying to find her way. The trail was right here, she knew it. Beneath the canopy of trees, what little light there was coming from the sky had vanished. She bumped into stumps, smacked into branches. Finally, she found what seemed to be the trail. If it wasn't the trail, too bad. She had no choice. Franklin was coming, and she knew he wasn't far behind.

Her steps were short. Every few feet she would stumble, but she caught herself and pressed on.

God, she was *cold.* Her entire body trembled. She couldn't feel her hands or feet. *Better cold than dead,* she kept telling herself. *Better cold than dead. Better cold than—*

As she drew closer to Stevenson's cabin, she could see a misty illumination from one of the outbuildings, glowing ghostly, ominous. She had thought the small house was dark, and she was relieved to find there was a light on, after all.

The work light, she thought. *It was on earlier today. Cliff had been working on his truck when . . . .*

Anne ran now, ran out of the forest and into the small yard, toward the dark cabin.

Suddenly she was cannon-balled to the ground, her wind knocked completely from her lungs. A searing pain came from her foot, and she yelped.

No, please! No! No!

She rolled on the ground, clutching her leg. She'd tripped over something in the dark, or stepped in a small hole, twisting her ankle like a pretzel. Her foot was on fire. It ached, it throbbed. It burned like she'd dipped it in acid.

She struggled to her feet, and put a small amount of weight on her foot. The pain shot up her leg, worse than ever.

Oh, God. Just a little help. That's all I'm asking for. Just a little help here, okay?

She hopped on one leg to the dark cabin. Every jolting movement sent a pulse of gnawing pain through her. When she reached the porch she sat down, instantly snapping up one of the softball-sized rocks that Stevenson placed around the foundations. She scrambled up on one leg, turned toward the house, and let the rock fly.

It smashed the window of the door, and shrieking glass scattered. Anne turned around, looking and listening for signs of Franklin. She heard nothing but her own heart slamming beneath her breasts.

Again, she tried to put some weight on her injured foot; again, it screamed at her.

She struggled up the porch by sitting on it, swinging both legs up, then climbing to one leg, leaning on the doorjamb for support. Jagged pieces of glass remained in the broken window. She pulled the large ones out carefully and tossed them aside. They sailed into the air and took wing like shiny, glistening bats, then tumbled down and sliced into the grass.

Reaching in the window, she turned her arm down and fumbled with the lock. She turned the button easily, and with her other hand, she turned the knob from the outside. The knob rotated, and the door opened with an oh-so-welcome, comforting *ka-clunk*.

Thank you, God. I won't forget that one. Promise.

She pulled her arm back through the broken window, drew the door open, and slipped inside.

fifty five

She flipped on a light—and the first thing she saw was a gun. A big shotgun over the fireplace mantle. Double-barrel Remington, twelve-gauge. Hope took wings.

She drew the curtain closed, hobbled across the floor and pulled the gun down, cracking the barrels open.

Empty.

Shit. It would have been too good to be true, anyway.

But he'd have ammunition somewhere. Or maybe another gun. One that was loaded.

Carrying the shotgun, she limped down the hall and into a bedroom as quickly as she could with her injured foot, knowing that it wouldn't take Mark Franklin long to reach the cabin. She turned on the bedroom light.

On the other side of the bed, a dark oak gun cabinet stood.

Full.

Stevenson had an assortment of everything: shotguns, rifles, even an old musket. Weapons lined the inside of the cabinet like steel soldiers. He was his own militia, for crying out loud. At least, he was while he had been alive. Hope was at ten thousand feet—and climbing.

She hopped to the cabinet, using the shotgun as a crutch. The glass doors were locked. Without an instant of hesitation, she drew back and plunged the stock of the Remington through the glass. It shattered in a hailstorm of slivers and shards. The arsenal was now at her disposal. Hope hit the stratosphere—then came crashing to the ground as she checked the guns. First, the shotgun.

Empty.

Then a Winchester 30-30, and a Weatherby Mark V.

Empty.

None of the guns were loaded. There was no ammunition in any chamber, and none in the cabinet.

Cliff, where did you keep it?!?! her mind screamed. She tore through dressers, looked under the bed. Nothing.

She hobbled to the kitchen, frantically sweeping through cupboards. Into the living room, under the couch, everywhere.

Her efforts were unrewarded, and her mind was swirling. The pain in her foot brought constant anguish, and the frustration of not being able to find any ammunition was overwhelming. All the while, *Bestseller* kept nudging back to her mind. It was like a stray dog, scratching at the door, wanting to be let in. *Scratch, scratch. Here I am. Let me in? Pause. Wait. Scratch, scratch. I'm still here.*

She looked out the door, into the dark night, and her spirits sank even further.

A light. Over by the stream.

He was coming.

But which way was he going to go? Would he go back to her cabin . . . or come here, to Stevenson's?

She quickly clicked off the living room light and poked her head out the door again. Franklin's light was strong. She could see the forest around him, illuminated in the super-intense glare.

And he was moving. He was coming this way.

Toward Stevenson's cabin.

fifty six

The weight of her situation pressed down on her, nearly snuffing out all hope. The helplessness, the pain in her foot. She knew she couldn't run now; it was impossible. Her ankle was broken, or, at the very least, sprained badly.

I can't run. He's got me now. I can hide here in the house, but he'll find me. He'll find me and he

walked toward the bed with several small alligator clips. Wires dangled from the tiny metal jaws. They were connected to a small box on the dresser. He affixed the clips to the safety-pin piercings.

"Beth, what I'm going to do to you is shocking. Just . . . shocking. Let me know how it floats your boat." He flipped the switch, and immediately

Floats your boat? Floats your boat?

Still standing in the doorway, she looked out over the lake. On the other side, the lights from her cabin glowed on the polished surface. Stars gleamed, reflecting on the flat water. Near the shore, not far from where she stood, Cliff's rowboat sat at the end of the dock, enveloped by shadows.

No, I can't run . . . but I can row! Row out into the lake. That's not in the book. It's not part of the story. He won't expect it. And I'll keep the shotgun. He won't know that it's empty.

Using the shotgun as a cane, she limped down the short slope and onto the dock. The old boards groaned beneath her and she untied the boat from its moorings. One foot in, then two. The boat moaned beneath her weight, rolling gently to and fro. Anne sat in the middle, placed the shotgun next to her, and grasped the oars. She pushed off from the dock.

Made it. God. I made it.

She rowed as softly as she could. Maybe he wouldn't hear her. Maybe . . . *maybe* . . . he wouldn't see her. The old aluminum squeaked with every move she made, and even the tiniest peep seemed to boom like thunder.

Maybe, if I'm quiet enough, he won't know I'm out here. I can row to the middle of the lake and drift.

She rowed slowly, pulling the oars easily, bringing the blades from the water silently, then repeating the motion. All the while she watched Franklin's light sweeping through the forest, heading down the trail to Stevenson's cabin. With each pull of the oars, a tiny bud of hope glimmered. Not much of a glimmer, but kind of a pilot-light. Just a drop of fire, but at least it was something.

Her eyes adjusted to the dark. There were two fishing poles in the boat. One was on the side, next to her, the other behind her, hanging over the bow. And on the floor behind her seat—

A tackle box. A big one, the size of an Amana microwave. She stopped rowing and let the oars hang in the water.

Fishermen carry tackle, spare line, hooks . . . and knives.

She quietly opened up the box and peered inside. All she could see were shadows.

She placed her hand in the box and was bitten immediately. A Heddon *Jitterbug.* Lethal for bass; painful to humans when hooked. The sharp point pierced her skin, but it hadn't gone passed the barb. She carefully extracted the treble hook from her palm and returned the lure to the tray.

She placed her hand in the box again, slower this time. Several more pokes, but nothing serious. She found a pair of pliers, fingernail clippers, several plastic bobbers. She found no knife.

At the bottom of the tackle box was yet another container. Rectangular, and made of metal. Nearly as big as a shoe box. She moved her hand over it, feeling the ridges of the design on the top. A big plus sign. First Aid Kit.

She removed the kit from the bottom of the tackle box and held it in her lap. The latch was old and rusted. The kit hadn't been used in a long time, if ever.

The lid flipped open. Her hands found gauze pads of assorted sizes, bandages, tape. A small bottle of something, probably ointment or antibacterial cream. And some kind of tool at the bottom of the kit. It was heavy, and Anne pulled it out and held it in her hands, held it up to the sky to see its silhouette.

No, not a tool. Not a tool at all.

A flare gun.

fifty seven

"Annie . . . I know where you aaaaare."

Mark Franklin's sing-song voice echoed over the lake, disturbing the serenity. Although she was a good distance from him, there were no other sounds, no natural barriers to drown out his speech. He had reached Stevenson's cabin and was shining the light in the windows. She had fooled him; he thought she was at Stevenson's. He thought that she was hiding inside. She felt good, and, for a moment at least, allowed herself the satisfaction. Years ago, Mick Jagger sang that he could get none; Anne Harper just had a double dose.

The light continued to flash around Stevenson's cabin. She heard his voice again, still sing-songy and taunting. "I know where you are, Anne, because I planned it that way. It's all going according to plan."

Bullshit. I screwed up your plan when I jumped out of the car. She remained perfectly still, perfectly silent. The boat drifted in the middle of the lake. A sliver of moon rose in the east like a glowing scimitar. Stars winked back at her from the glassy water.

"It'll be over soon, Annie." His voice reverberated through the dark forest and across the lake. But there were new emotions in his voice: tension. *Anger.* His game wasn't going exactly the way he had planned it, and he was growing impatient.

And he was moving. He's moving toward the cabin. My cabin!

And he was. She watched the light swing, and she could hear faint snaps and pops of branches crunching as he walked. She had fooled him, and he was *pissed.* She knew he was.

Score one for Annie, she thought. *Certainly not a major victory, but another notch on the wall. One for the home team.*

The light was moving fast now. She could hear branches snapping, and heavy plodding. He was running.

Anne's mind whirred with possible scenarios.

If he finds me on the lake he could get the rowboat from my cabin. He could come get me.

No. Then she'd be able to row to the opposite side of the lake. *He won't let that happen. He doesn't know that I can't run.*

Another thought:

I could row back to Stevenson's cottage. Now that he's on the other side of the lake, I could make it to his cabin.

Too risky. Besides . . . what would she do when she got there? If he knew that's where she was going, he'd have time to run to the cabin before she got there. And there were no other trails, nothing anywhere near the lake.

Whichever way she looked at it, it was a game of hide and seek. A waiting game. The safest place she could be is in a rowboat in the middle of the lake. She could wait here all night. Till tomorrow. She was expected back in New York in the morning. When she hadn't arrived, there would be phone calls. Someone would be sent to check on her. When? Who knows. But when she hadn't arrived, Candace would get worried. She'd make some phone calls, do some checking. Send someone to look for her? It seemed more than she could hope for, but right now, it was one more item in her Wishful Thinking bag . . . which was pretty empty for the time being.

The shotgun would be useless unless he saw that she had it. Then he might think it was loaded. It was dangerous play, for sure, but it was an option. It was something that wasn't written in the book.

And she had the flare gun. She'd never used one before. It was old, and might not even work. But it was still another item for her Wishful Thinking bag.

Across the lake at her cabin, a silhouette crossed the yard. Franklin's dark figure stalked slowly around the small cottage.

Guess again, you sick bastard.

He vanished into the shadows. Anne watched, her heart pounding.

What next?

An owl hooted in the forest. It was the first sound she'd heard all night, besides the very faint whirring of crickets on shore. The owl's cry was haunting, lonely.

Mark will go into the cabin. He'll find I'm not there. He'll think I've tried to run. Then he'll—

A door slammed heavily, pounding over the lake. Franklin emerged from the cabin, his dark form stalking toward the lake.

"ANNIE!" he shouted. The tension in his voice had elevated. "ANNIE! I KNOW WHERE YOU ARE!"

No you don't. If you did you wouldn't be yelling. I messed up your plans.

When the light clicked on, it reminded her of the beginning of a 20th Century Fox movie. Right at the beginning, before the opening credits, where thick searchlights sweep the sky.

The beam hit the trees at the edge of the lake. It was like fire. The entire area was lit up. The brilliant laser swept down to the surface of the water, then cut a swath across the lake, illuminating the trees on the adjacent side. It swung slowly, coming toward her, closer. She ducked down below the gunwhale, crouching low.

Shit. Shit. Shit . . .

Suddenly, the boat was bathed in a white glow. Anne swore she could actually feel the heat of the searchlight.

Please keep going, she thought. *Maybe he can't see this far out into the lake.* There was another one for the Wishful Thinking bag.

Suddenly, he called to her again in that pathetic, childish sing-song.

"I seeeeeee yoooo, Annie . . . ."

Her Wishful Thinking bag spilled its contents all over the bottom of the boat. He'd spotted her.

But that was okay. *She* was okay. For now. He was there, she was here. She was in the boat, he was on shore. He wasn't going to swim. And if he tried rowing? Well, she had a good head start. She could make it to the other side of the lake. She'd be on shore while he'd still be rowing.

Problem is, Annie, she thought, *you're crippled. When you hit land, you're not going very far.*

A sudden spray of water several feet away jolted her. The spray showered her and she jumped, confused. It was followed instantly by a loud, echoing *crack!* that boomed over the lake.

A gunshot. Franklin had a gun.

fifty eight

Anne's thoughts flashed. Another splash, followed instantly by the sharp report of the gun. Then a loud *rrriiipp* shook the boat, and she could actually feel the force of the bullet as it tore open the aluminum hull.

"You can't go anywhere, Anne," he called out. His last words bounced across the lake, and Anne heard her name several times before it faded completely. Another splash, another acute explosion from the gun severed the night.

The next bullet hit the boat again, near the bow. The bullet tore through the old aluminum as easily as it would have pierced a loaf of bread. Anne grasped the oars and tried to crouch down and row at the same time. From the shore, Mark Franklin continued to taunt her.

"I like moving targets, Annie. It's more sporting that way."

The light was still trained on her. She knew she was lit up like a roman candle. Still, she rowed frantically, trying desperately to get out of the beam, to put more distance between her and Franklin.

Another sudden jolt rocked the boat, and her right arm shuddered as the blade of the oar splintered. She swung it back and forth, but it pushed no water. It was useless. Now she could row all she wanted and all she'd be doing is rowing in circles.

Another splash, another gunshot. If she was going to live, she'd have to swim for it.

But to where? If she swam to Stevenson's cabin, he'd follow the trail and get there before she did. Besides . . . with her ankle in the condition it was, outrunning him wasn't something she'd be able to do.

The only other option would be the north shore. Find a place to hide, to stay. She was closer to *that* shore, anyway. But it was thickly wooded and swampy. The forest was marshy, and spiny alders grew like thatchwork. Which wouldn't make it any easier for her, but her options were gone. If she was going to hide in the woods, that would be the place to do it.

Still another splash, another gunshot. Anne scooped up the flare gun from the seat. Whether or not it would work after it had gotten wet, she didn't know. But it was the only item left in her Wishful Thinking bag; she was going to hang on to it. The shotgun, unfortunately, had only proved useful as a temporary crutch. She'd have to leave it behind.

With a single motion, she rolled over the edge of the boat and into the water.

The extreme cold took her breath away. She'd been chilled already; now she felt like she'd been plunged into a vat of ice water. It was especially cold to her head, and it felt like a knife had been plunged into her temple.

She surfaced, tried to touch bottom. Nope. She knew the lake was supposed to be deep; just how deep, she didn't know. The light was still trained on the boat, but she was on the opposite side, in the shadow of the hull.

"No fair, Annie," Franklin's voice echoed. "Beth never used a boat in the book."

The stalker never had a gun in the book, either, she thought. *And besides . . . I'm not going by your damned book, Franklin.*

The flare gun was in her hand, beneath the surface. There was no way she could swim with it. Swimming with one hand and grasping the gun with the other was too cumbersome. And it was too big to put in the pocket of her pants.

With one hand on the gunwhale of the boat, she shoved the flare gun entirely down the front of her jeans. The bulging object pressed against her belly and pinched at her skin. But both of her hands were free.

She began to swim in the shadow of the boat, slowly, quietly. She knew he couldn't see her. If she traveled back far enough, she could slip out from the shadow and turn to her right, north, and head for shore without being seen.

Franklin was silent. No more gunshots, no more shouting. He swept the beam back and forth across the lake. As long as the boat remained between them, Franklin wouldn't be able to see her.

The light clicked off.

If she was going to make it to the north shore, if she was going to have any chance of getting away from this lunatic, it was now.

She turned, and began swimming for the north shore.

fifty nine

She wasn't playing his way, and Franklin was *pissed.* He'd hoped that maybe, *maybe* when he started firing at her, she'd give up. Throw in the towel. She was a sitting duck, after all. Even she had to know that.

But he didn't want to shoot her. That wouldn't be fun. The story had come so far, they had been through so many chapters already. Sure, a few chapters had been added, but, all in all, the plot remained intact. The story still held.

And Anne Harper wasn't going anywhere. This was just a minor adjustment, a new twist to the story.

But now she was swimming. Son of a bitch. *What in the hell was she trying to do? Where did she think she was going?*

He clicked off the light. *Okay, Anne. We'll play it your way this chapter. Either way, the story stays the same.*

Franklin removed the bag from his shoulder, ran down to the dock, and leapt into the rowboat. He would easily be able to overtake her. He placed the rifle and the light on the seat, grabbed the oars, and began stroking. The boat churned past the end of the dock. Franklin took long, powerful sweeps with the oars, and the boat moved quickly out into the lake, skimming the surface like a skater.

He paused to grab the light. He clicked it on, sweeping the beam across the water.

There. There's the boat. She can't be far. He turned the light off and continued rowing.

Sixty seconds later, he again dropped the oars and turned the light on. Stevenson's boat floundered only a few yards away. He waved the searchlight back and forth, listening. He could hear splashing, could hear her in the water. He aimed the light in the direction of the sound, sweeping it back and forth, back and forth—

There. He could see her crawling arm over arm, swimming away from him. *She's headed for the north shore. To the swamp. Bad move, Annie. The woods are too thick. You won't go two feet.*

He would be upon her in less than a minute. He was happy, he was smiling inside. Everything was coming together. She might make it to shore. Might. But then what? Where would she go? She couldn't. Not without a light.

And even then, the forest was so thick she'd need a machete to get through.

No, the last few chapters of the story were going to go as planned, like he knew they would. The last few chapters were going to be spine-tinglers. Real chiller-dillers.

Plop, swish. Plop, swish. He pulled the oars harder, forcing the boat across the surface of the dark water. Every few seconds he paused and held the oars, listening.

He was getting close now. He could hear her struggling in the water, could hear her gasping for breath. He kept rowing.

Plop, swish. Plop, swish. Pause.

He turned. He was so close now that even in the darkness, he could see her shadow thrashing in the water. She was only a dozen feet from shore.

Nice try, Annie. Nice try. He shouldered the rifle, then reached for the light.

sixty

She knew that he was getting close.

Anne could hear the oars pushing water, the banging of aluminum, and Franklin's heavy breathing. But she didn't dare turn around. It would waste too much time. She focused on making it to shore. What would she do then?

Don't know. Don't know. Just get away from him. Get to shore. Her throbbing ankle was a constant reminder that, once she reached land, flight would be impossible.

The boat was very close now. Franklin couldn't be more than a few boat lengths away.

She wasn't going to make it. She knew it.

Her injured foot hit bottom, and she nearly cried out. She was surprised to find that she was in water that was only waist deep. She immediately planted her good foot and stood, trying to run. Maybe she could make it. Maybe—

A brilliant sun lit up from behind her. The trees on the shore exploded fiery white; her own shadow was monstrous upon the towering cedars. Even the water glowed like burning sulphur.

It was over. She'd nearly made it to shore. She'd nearly gotten away. Now, Franklin was behind her by only a few yards. There would be no more running now. No more swimming. She knew that the gun was trained on her, that if she so much as flinched, she'd be history. End of story.

"Anne."

She heard him speak but didn't acknowledge him. She just stared, gasping for breath, facing her shadow that covered the trees at the shore. Frigid water dripped from her chin.

"Anne. Turn around."

Slowly, she turned and faced the light. She squinted, and began to raise her arm to shield her eyes.

"No!" he ordered. "Stop. Don't move." Anne held her arm where it was. Water ran down to her elbow and dripped away. "Interesting chapter, Anne. Different. You really had me going, there. But it's time to get back to the original story."

The light was blinding. She couldn't see his face, his body, or even the boat. Everything was hot-white.

The light slowly drew nearer as the boat came closer.

"Grab the front of the boat, and back up," he said. "Slowly. Back up toward the shore."

She did as he asked, taking the front of the boat with one hand. The aluminum was cold. She took a step back, then another. Pain from her foot rocketed to her brain.

The bottom of the lake was soft and squishy, and her feet sank down to her ankles. Soft silt wormed between her toes. When she was knee-deep, he spoke again.

"Get in. You're going to row."

The light was still trained on her face. It was hot, like the bulbs of a tanning booth. She made out another form, a long barrel. The gun. It was aimed at her head. She knew that once she got in the boat, it was all over. Sure, she still had the flare gun. But even that was useless now. She was staring down the barrel of a rifle.

Slowly, she lifted her injured leg and swung it up over the side of the boat. Images rushed back to her, images from the book and what the stalker had done to Beth Huston. Only now, she saw Mark Franklin. And *she,* Anne Harper, was Beth Huston. She saw him as he

returned from the fireplace, a tiny, glowing ember held in the pinchers of a pair of needle-nose pliers. The coal was small, the size of a button. He waved the coal over her head, over her face, pausing to hold it over one eye. He paused, watching her reaction. If he dropped it now, at this very second, it would land directly into her eyeball. And it would be an easy target with both eyes bulging out the way they were.

He drew the orange coal away from her face, holding it over her neck, her breasts . . . .

Yes. Now there's an idea.

He lowered the coal, slowly, watching her facial expressions, watching her as the ember came closer to her skin. Her eyes ballooned as they followed the fiery, orange lump as it wavered above her breasts. Inches, *inches . . .*

He dropped the burning coal on her nipple. Beth tried to scream, tried to

Anne shook the thought away. *That* was not going to happen. Not to her. That was *not* the way the book would end. He was going to have to shoot her. A quick kill, and it would be all over.

"Take the middle seat. Move slow."

Anne only had one foot in the boat. She was about to remove it, to stand there defiantly and tell Franklin to just *do it, do it right now. There is no way I'm going back to that cabin. You're a sick freak of humanity, a disgusting, perverted pig. Worse.*

The light was still in her face, the barrel of the gun aimed at her head. Franklin shifted, and he stood up to move to the seat at the stern . . . .

An idea came to her.

Change of plans.

With all of her might, with every ounce of strength she had left, she seized the bow of the boat. At the same time, she pushed with her leg that was still straddled over the gunwhale. The pain from her injured foot shattered her nerves like a hand grenade, and she cried out.

But the effect was immediate. The boat bobbed violently, rocking sideways and backwards in a single, swift motion. The sudden jolt hadn't been enough to capsize the boat, or even draw in water over the sides. However, in that split instant, the beam of light shot up to the sky. A white needle speared into the night, tapering off into the stars. The rifle detonated with an ear-splitting concussion. Water erupted like a nuclear geyser at Anne's side, spraying her. She screamed—but the bullet had missed. It had struck the surface only inches from her leg. The shaft of light suddenly swayed back, falling, falling . . . .

There was a loud splash as Franklin hit the water. The light disappeared below the surface, but it still glowed brightly, its beam cutting a swath like a thick laser.

And she fled. The muck pulled at her feet, the water sloshed to her sides. Pain be damned. She had a *chance.* One more chance. She scrambled toward the dark border of cedars that crowded the shore.

The shore! I'll follow the shore back! I'll follow—

"You goddamn *bitch! You're DEAD, Annie! You are fucking dead! Beth Huston was nothing compared to what I'm going to do to you, Anne!*" Water splashed.

And there was something in his voice that was insanely *real.* He meant every word he said. Anne was certain that the pain that had been inflicted upon Beth Huston was only a *fraction* of what he would do to her.

The water was up to her knees. She couldn't run, but she was putting more and more distance between her and Franklin. Time was nonexistent. Only a few seconds had lapsed since Franklin had fallen into the water, but the short span had vanished. The past no longer existed. There was only right *now.* And the *future,* the next second, and the second after that. Anne needed every single one.

The light was on her again. The rifle cracked and she dove, only to emerge again, struggling to her feet.

Jesus. He's still got the gun. And the light. The light—

—blinked off.

Then on, then off. It remained off. She heard Franklin cursing. The rifle rang out again, but the water exploded several feet from where she was. He was guessing. He was guessing, damn it. *He couldn't see her!*

Trudging through the knee-deep water was exhausting and maddeningly painful. With every step, thick sludge pulled at her shoes, and she had to struggle harder just to pull her foot from the soft bottom. Every time she put weight on her injured foot, every time she had to pull it from the mud, she was jolted with excruciating pain. And the flare gun. *God.* That thing was killing her. When she walked, it jabbed into her pelvis. Without stopping, Anne pulled it out and carried it in hand.

She looked up and saw the light of the cabin. *Her* cabin. She focused on the dining room light.

Fifty yards. Fifty yards max. I can do it. I can make it.

sixty one

He struggled to get into the boat, but the water was over his waist. The powerful light had become waterlogged and quit working. He threw it into the water and began dragging the rowboat to shallower water. With every second that passed, he could hear Anne sloshing further and further away.

Will not. Not get away. Bitch. BITCH! He threw a leg up over the side of the rowboat and leapt inside, crashing to the middle bench. He placed the rifle on the seat and reached for the oars—

Where the fuck is . . . .

He grasped one oar with his left hand, but the other oar was gone. He felt the seat. *No!* He looked around, in the water.

The oar was gone. He had knocked it out of the oarlock when he'd fallen.

He snapped up the rifle and blindly fired off a shot in the direction of Anne's sloshing. Then he leapt from the boat, landing feet first in the water. Another shot in her direction, only this time it was a sidearm shot, while he pushed through the water.

No more talking. No more shouting. He was raging like a tornado. Anne was going to die. There was nowhere she could go. He would hunt her like an animal, then—

Play it by the book. Just like the book. No . . . worse.

The water was numbing cold, but he never felt it. His feet sucked into the mud. Water pushed against his legs. He could hear Anne ahead of him, pushing through the water. Every so often he caught a quick glimpse of her dark profile in the glowing light from the cabin. He aimed in her direction, fired off a shot, missed. He pressed on.

Louder splashing. *Faster* splashing, and then it ceased. Anne's silhouette appeared in the light of the cabin. She had made it to shore, and she was racing toward the small cottage.

He shouldered the rifle, aimed quickly, fired. Glass exploded. He fired again.

Anne fell.

He lowered the rifle.

She got up and continued toward the cabin, but—

She's limping. Fuckin'-a she is. Got her in the leg. She won't be going anywhere.

He muscled through the thigh-deep water, watching Anne as she reached the cabin and disappeared inside.

Perfect. There's a death wish, Annie. It's where I was going to bring you in the first place.

In less than a minute, he, too, was at the shore. His pace had slowed, and he moved easier, more carefree. After all, Anne was in the cabin. She had no place to go, no car to drive, no weapons besides a few measly knives and a fire poker. He had a *rifle.*

Top that, Annie-bitch.

He retrieved his shoulder bag from where he'd left it in the grass. With one arm he kept the rifle to his shoulder, aiming, staring down the barrel, finger coiled around the trigger.

He strode arrogantly up to the cabin. All of the lights were on now. The curtains were still closed.

And Anne was inside.

The dining room window had shattered, struck by a stray shot. Part of the curtain had been shredded by glass, and he could see through the torn fabric and inside the cottage, inside the living room, part of the hall, and—

Anne. She was seated on the wood floor. He couldn't see much, just a portion of her denim jeans, and a pool of water that had formed at her ankles and buttocks.

And her hand. She had the iron fireplace poker in her hand. He could see its arrow-shaped tip, with a curved barb that looped back around like a gigantic fishhook.

"Oh, Annie, Annie, Annie," he called softly. *"Little orphan Annie, all alone. Do you wanna play? I've got a few really fun games for you, Anne. I think you'll like them. I think you may have even read about them."*

Silence. He watched her through the curtain. She didn't move.

"You know what the funny thing is, Anne? Here we are. Here we are, the same place we would have wound up anyway. Of course, we were *supposed* to begin at the field like poor Beth Huston. You've tired us both out a bit, I'm afraid. But that's okay. I'm prepared for that. Because, Annie, since you've made this so . . . *difficult* . . . I'll be taking my time with you. I have a little something special that Gerald didn't write about in his book. You do know, don't you, that Gerald Morgan is the author of *Bestseller?*"

Silence. The only sounds were chirping crickets. No planes, no honking. No noise. Just crickets.

"Oh, yes. Morgan wrote the book. But I didn't like the way it ended. It was too rosy, too flowery, too . . . *happy*. It was also too *good* for someone like Morgan. So, I . . . *relieved* him of the responsibility, so to speak. Along with a few other things, such as his shoes, which I'm wearing, and several of his kitchen knives. When you're found here, the trail will lead right to our good friend Gerald Morgan.

"But *Bestseller* needed work. So I had to revise it a bit, put some finishing touches on it. And three hours from now, you'll be wishing you were Beth Huston. Oh, yes, you're going to live longer than her. Longer than Beth did. I'm going to make you feel things you've never felt before. *I'll make you scream and scream . . . the way I made Caroline Yates scream.*"

sixty two

Oh God, Anne thought. *No. Was it possible? Mark Franklin was the one who—*

"You see, Anne, I had always wanted to be a novelist. A book writer. But I never got anywhere. I sent out dozens of letters to publisher after publisher, agent after agent, and nobody paid attention. And when I met Caroline Yates, well, a certain idea popped into my head. It was a *good* idea. I decided that if I couldn't write a book that anyone seemed to want, well, then, I would simply borrow someone else's."

She could hear his voice through the dining room window, and she backed further into the hall.

"That someone was—"

"You're lying."

"Oh? She speaks?" he taunted from outside the shattered window. "Yes, I'm afraid it's true. I simply borrowed Caroline Yates's story. No one read it, as you are aware. You were her agent. She never let anyone read her stories. You were always the first, weren't you?"

Anne didn't answer.

"I waited a few months after her death, and then submitted my wonderful work to you. Which, if I remember your personal phone call, you stated that my book was simply *heartstopping*. Funny how you used that word."

Anne remembered. She remembered receiving the manuscript, remembered reading the entire work in one sitting, staying up until three in the morning. She remembered wanting to call Mark Franklin right then and there. And yes, she had told him that *Theater of the Mine* was *heartstopping*.

"Success was wonderful. Book signings around the country, fame, money. It was great. But you wouldn't represent any of my future books, Anne. You said they 'weren't for you'. In essence, you fired me, Anne. You killed my career."

Anne's mind spiraled. She couldn't believe it. Wouldn't believe it. Yet, now that she thought about it, Caroline Yates very easily could have penned *Theater of the Mine*. And Anne had been surprised, time and time again, whenever Franklin had submitted a new manuscript. It was like they had been penned by a third-grader.

Like . . . his first book had been written by someone else.

Anne trembled on the floor, gripping the poker. She looked over at the stove, at the pot of water over the blue flame. *Keep him talking. Keep him talking.*

"I didn't do a thing, Mark. Your stories weren't—"

"Acceptable? Is that the problem, Annie Harper? They were . . . *Un*-acceptable?"

"They were—"

"Tell me," he interrupted in that same mocking, pious manner, "tell me how you liked the last few chapters of *Bestseller.*"

She paused.

Tell him what? That he was an inherently evil, cruel, sick person? That he was insane? What? Tell him what?

"Well? What did you think, Anne?"

Tell him something. She looked at the pot on the stove, calculating how long it would take for the water to boil. *Tell him anything . . . just keep him talking.*

"I think with some editing—"

"Oh please, Annie!" His tone was now sarcastic, biting. "You, of *all* people, know that it is madness! It's ruthless, it's atrocious. It's barbaric." Sweeter now: "It's . . . it's—*justice.*"

"Justice?!?!" Anne heard herself shouting. *"For what? What kind of justice do you call that?!?!?"*

"Poetic, Anne. *Poetic* justice. You see, when I couldn't get another book published, I ran out of money. We lost our home. I lost my wife and children. Traveling around the country allowed me to pursue certain . . . *interests,* if you will.

A particular hobby that I'd grown fond of. I lost everything because of you."

The water on the stove began to simmer.

Yes, Franklin. Keep talking. Keep talking.

"I got a first-hand look at how the publishers treat their authors, Anne. How agents treat their authors. You are only out for yourself, Anne. You and everyone else in the business."

"That's bullshit, and you know it."

"Is it? You can level with me now, Anne, can't you? Or have you lied so much to so many people that you just can't tell the truth anymore?"

Anne spoke, anxiously eyeing the pot on the stove. "If it doesn't work for the author, it doesn't work for *anyone*. Myself included. *Everybody* has to win."

"I don't buy that, Anne. And you don't, either. A handful of writers make money. The rest . . . well, they get thrown to the dogs. They get treated the way poor Beth Huston was treated. But I'm getting tired of explaining, Anne."

The thin rifle barrel slid slowly through the broken window, hidden behind the shredded curtains. Anne didn't see it.

"We have a long night ahead of us, Ms. Harper. There are many things we'll be doing, you and I. Might as well get started."

A sudden explosion erupted and, simultaneously, the cast-iron pot on the stove was blown across the kitchen, spilling scalding water all over the floor, the walls, the ceiling. Water doused the gas burner with a steaming hiss, and the blue flame went out. The hobbled iron pot clanged like a caged bee, slamming against the counter and cabinets, then tumbling to the floor. The outburst caused Anne's entire body to shudder, and she quickly scrambled closer to the bedroom. From outside the dining room window, Franklin withdrew the rifle and spoke.

"Annie . . . just what did you think you were going to do with that?"

Footsteps pounded around the cabin, and there were two heavy pounds at the door as Franklin slammed it with the butt of the rifle.

Jesus! He's coming in! He's coming inside!

A third pound ripped the entire lock and the deadbolt mechanism from the doorjamb. Wood splintered and cracked, and the entire cabin shook as the door exploded.

sixty three

Anne scrambled into the bedroom, holding the poker, already knowing that, against a rifle, her own weapon was pretty much useless. But she wasn't willing to give it up. She wasn't going down without one hell of a fight. She'd be damned if she was going to let him do those things to her. He would have to kill her first.

Unless . . . .

It was her very last chance. Her *only* chance. The only item left in her Wishful Thinking bag.

"Annie . . . *I'm home.*" Haughty laughter. Slow footsteps. "My Nicholson needs work, I know," he sneered.

Anne backed against the far wall in the bedroom, on the other side of the bed. The bedroom door was open, and

Mark Franklin's shadow appeared in the hall. He stopped before she could see him.

"Splendid, Anne. My favorite room in the house. That must mean you're ready."

She remained frozen, standing against the wall, favoring her injured foot. Her heart was slamming, her pulse racing. She held the iron poker like a baseball bat.

The shadow moved, grew larger. Fast. No sneaking this time. Franklin was moving.

And then: he was in the doorway. He shouldered the rifle with one arm, finger looped around the trigger. In his other hand was a large grocery bag-sized satchel. He placed it on the floor at his feet.

"Oh, Anne," he said, seeing her stance with the poker. "That's not one of the games we'll be playing."

"You'll have to kill me, Mark."

He laughed. "Oh, I will, I will. That's the plan. But that's going to be a while, I'm afraid. You see, I've got a little something special. Something that I didn't include in *Bestseller*."

He kept the rifle aimed at her, reached into his bag, and removed a digital camera. "To capture the moment in pictures," he said. "Don't want to let these wonderful memories pass us by."

He placed the camera on the dresser and again reached into the bag. Franklin pulled out a sealed sandwich bag containing a small amount of white powder.

"Cocaine," he said, holding up the bag. "It's marvelous, really. It serves several purposes. First, it will help keep us both awake. We'll need our strength tonight, and I wouldn't want you to . . . fall asleep on me.

"Secondly, it is the most marvelous pain reliever known to man. For example, when I slice your nipple off like a pepperoni, I'm sure you'll feel some discomfort. But I'll be *kind,* Anne. I'll place some coke on the . . . *affected* area, and the pain will go away, allowing you to bear many more fun activities. Of course, the drug wears off after a while, but those are the breaks. Are you ready?"

"I said you'll have to kill me." She glared straight at him. Her voice shook, and her whole body trembled. She was looking straight at the barrel of the rifle.

"No, Anne. That's not what you want. It's too messy." He aimed the gun at her foot. "I'll wound you until you drop that poker, Anne. Then, I'll stop the bleeding and take care of you. And believe me . . . *I know how to take care of you."*

She wanted to scream. She wanted to kill him. This was a nightmare, a sick, perverted dream. It couldn't be real. Couldn't be.

Hands trembling, she slowly lowered the poker to the bed.

sixty four

"Good girl," Franklin said, still shouldering the rifle. He leaned forward and grasped the poker, pulled it off the bed, and threw it down the hall. It banged off the wall and clanged to a halt in the kitchen. He smiled. "We'll be using that later, as I'm sure you know. Now. Take off your clothes. I want to see you. I want to see you now."

Anne didn't move. Her hands were trembling, and her legs shook. She was no longer aware of the painful throbbing of her foot.

"Anne?"

Slowly, she pulled up her shirt and brought it up over her head.

"Give it to me."

She tossed the shirt to him. He stared at her with a glazed smile, his eyes moving up and down her body. "You look lovely, Anne. Beautiful. You *really* do. Now . . . the bra. Slow." He lowered the rifle and leaned it against the wall by the door. She was going nowhere, he knew. He had won.

Hands trembling, Anne slowly reached around her back to unsnap her bra. Her left hand found the clasp, and she held it between her fingers. She looked at his face, realizing that this was not Mark Franklin that stood before her. Oh it *was* Mark Franklin, in a manner of speaking. But here, now, his face was almost unrecognizable. His face was waxy, his features mannequin-like. It was as if he had taken on an entirely different persona, and his face looked as if he had somehow molded and changed it. She couldn't tell, exactly. But she knew that the man that stood before her, on the other side of the bed, was not the man he'd led so many people to believe he was.

"Anne, dear? I'm waiting. And while I could stay and watch you stand there all night, we do have . . . *work to do.*"

Her fingers twisted, and there was a very light *snap* as her bra strap unhinged.

One chance. One shot. One chance.

In one swift motion, her right hand shot down, reaching into the back of her jeans. Her bra slipped forward, exposing her breasts. Franklin went for his rifle—but Anne had already pulled the flare gun out from behind her.

"NO!" she screamed at him. She stumbled when she placed too much weight on her injured foot, but she caught

herself. *"DON'T . . . MOVE!"* She leveled the flare gun at him. He stopped, one hand on the rifle, his eyes darting from the flare gun, then back to Anne.

"Don't . . . move. I'll shoot, Mark. I swear to God I will." Her jaw tightened, and short breaths of air slipped in and out between her teeth.

Franklin flashed a confident grin.

"Annie . . . your voice is trembling. Are you alright?" He looked at the flare gun in her hand, and he slowly grasped the rifle. "Surely you wouldn't—"

Anne pulled the trigger.

Click. Franklin blinked, flinched a tiny bit.

Nothing happened. No *bang,* no thundering concussion of gunshot. No audience cheering for the hero. The flare gun was too old, had been at the bottom of Stevenson's tackle box far too long.

The roadrunner's anvil of despair pounded Anne into the ground. She felt dizzy and sick. It had been her last chance, her only hope. When Franklin had blown the boiling water from the stove, she'd tucked the flare gun into the back of her jeans. It was to be her last resort, her ace in the hole. The only thing left in her Wishful Thinking bag. Now, it was over. Everything was gone. She was gone, Caroline Yates was gone, Cliff Stevenson—

Goodbye, Allie. Goodbye, baby. She started to lower the flare gun.

"Oh, Anne. I'm sorry that—"

There was a sudden fizzling noise, a carbonated fizzing sound. A louder pop. Suddenly, the flare gun exploded, sending a shower of sparks and flame into the room . . . and a golfball-sized orb of fire directly into Mark Franklin's chest.

sixty five

The fiery meteor lodged between Franklin's shirt and skin. He screamed madly, sweeping the flaming ball away, pushing it from his body. The air reeked of burning hair and flesh. The ball of fire fell to the floor, bouncing a few times before it came to a stop where it continued to burn.

Anne leapt over the bed, only vaguely aware of the pain in her foot. She landed on top of Franklin and knocked him to the ground, then struggled to her feet.

"YOU BITCH!" he screamed *"YOU GODDAMN BITCH! YOU DIE! YOU DIE!"*

Anne whirled on her good leg. Franklin, still on the floor, reached out with his hand and grabbed her foot. Anne yelped as he twisted her injured leg. She fell to the floor, and pulled her foot from his grasp. She crawled on her hands and knees, then struggled to her feet again.

Franklin reached for the rifle, but it was too far away. Instead, his hand reached into the duffel bag and retrieved a foot-long knife. He bounded from the floor, held the knife high, and lunged. Anne tried to get away, tried to step aside, but her injured foot wouldn't let her move fast enough. She succeeded in making it down the hall and into the kitchen before Franklin caught up with her.

Bodies tumbled across the kitchen and crashed into the dining room table. *Bestseller* exploded like confetti, white pages billowing up and around, looping, falling.

Anne hit the floor and the bottle of merlot barely missed her head. It became a crimson missile, shattering next to her ear and sending glass shrapnel and red liquid everywhere. She felt the glass from the shattered window pierce her back in dozens of places. The warm wine soaked her hair and filled her ear.

Franklin was on top of her, and he drew up quickly and pulled back the knife.

"You bitch!" he screamed. *"You cunt! You fucking cunt!"* His arm came down at her, aiming the knife at her face. Anne shrieked, snapped her head to the side, feeling a sharp pain as a piece of the wine bottle cut her below her temple. The knife blade missed her cheek by inches. It stabbed the floor and Franklin pulled it back, readying for the next assault.

Anne saw part of the broken wine bottle, the neck, and she groped for it.

The broken wine bottle. Gotta get . . . gotta . . . .

Her hand flailed wildy. The stem of the bottle was intact, with sharp, angular edges.

Gotta get . . . .

The knife came down again. Again, she was able to move aside as the blade speared the wood floor. Franklin hadn't missed by much.

Her hand found the bottle neck, and she sliced her palm open on a sharp edge. The broken neck spun out of her grasp. She fumbled madly for it, for—

The compressed air wine opener. She felt it in her hand. Franklin had placed it on the table with the bottle of merlot.

The knife came down again in a blinding fury, burying itself into her flesh above her collarbone. The pain was caustic, dizzying. Anne screamed as the blade tore completely through her muscle, straight through her shoulder, and out the other side. The knife blade had literally pinned her to the floor.

With a sudden, adrenaline-charged burst she swung her arm around, gripping the wine bottle opener tightly, swinging with all of her strength, bringing the opener up and around, around—and burying the four-inch needle into the side of Franklin's head. It punctured his temple and pierced through solid bone. Anne forced it harder, boring through the skull and into Franklin's brain.

His body shook once, violently, like he'd been kicked in the ribs. He uttered a short, choking cough. Then he began to struggle, began to pull away, his movements shaky and uncontrolled. His hand still grasped the knife that was buried in her shoulder, and Anne winced as he tried to withdraw the blade. The steel dug her flesh, sending hot sparks of pain through her.

She pressed the button on the wine opener. There was a gentle hiss, like the slow opening of a soda bottle, and the compressed air was forced deep into his brain.

Franklin's body rocked in a sudden, turbulent seizure. Every muscle in his body tensed. Anne continued holding the button, afraid to let go, afraid that Franklin would remove the knife from her shoulder to bury it in her once again, only this time it would be her neck or her face. She kept the pressure on the opener, the four-inch needle buried in the back of his head. His ear was almost to her mouth and she spoke to him in a strained, forced whisper. *"I . . . am . . . re . . . writing . . . your . . . book . . . you . . . BASTARD!"*

Bubbles, all frothy-red, began to spew from the tiny entry hole in the side of Franklin's head. They sounded like the gurgling of air escaping from an inflated water toy.

Franklin stopped shaking, and his body went limp. His hand fell from the knife in Anne's shoulder. Hot saliva and bile dribbled from his mouth and onto Anne's neck. For another full minute, Anne held the button of the wine opener down, until the gentle hissing and bubbling stopped. The cannister was empty.

Mark Franklin was dead.

sixty six

"I'll take that call. I've gotta head out to Three Corners, anyway."

Sheriff Deputy Alfred Moore, aka 'Hunter,' picked up his hat. He'd had the nickname since childhood, when he shot a deer when he was eleven years old. He wasn't of legal age to hunt, but the Moore family wasn't all that well off, and a deer was a deer. It would put food in their stomachs during the long winter when work was scarce and money was even more scarce. People in the Upper Peninsula looked out for their own: they looked the other way at such discrepancies. Especially when it was an eleven year old kid helping to support his family. There was just something damned honorable about that.

A call had just came in from a woman in New York. Someone hadn't shown up when they were expected to. Staying at George Otto's cabin, on Lost Lake. Could someone go there and have a look?

A voice from the dispatch office down the hall acknowledged his departure and requested a coffee. "Black. Medium, with a lid."

"I'll be a while. Hour or so. Going to Otto's cabin."

There was a pause from the back room. Then: "Make it a large."

Moore left the station and climbed into the Suburban. Eight a.m., and the temperature was already seventy five degrees. It was going to be a hot one.

The drive to Three Corners took nearly half an hour. Plus, he'd stopped a kid on a four-wheeler without a helmet, putting him another ten minutes behind. Let him off with a warning. It was his good deed for the day.

He looked at the name on the slip of paper on the seat. *Anne Harper. Thirty-six, shoulder-length, blonde-brown hair. Supposed to have arrived in New York this morning, supposed to call last night.*

Hunter thought he'd probably be waking someone out of a perfectly sound sleep.

As he turned onto the dirt road that led to the two track that wound to Otto's cabin, the figure on the dirt road caught him by surprise. He stopped the vehicle.

And for the first time in his life, Hunter was speechless. Didn't swear, didn't say a word. Didn't even *think* it. There wasn't a single word or phrase to describe her, or the shape the woman was in. There was, of course. But words wouldn't come to Hunter.

It was *her*. The woman he was looking for. Had to be.

The woman saw the Suburban approaching and she had stopped, dead center in the middle of the dirt road. She was covered in blood. A red and black flannel shirt was draped carelessly over her shoulders, untucked and unbuttoned. Her hair was matted and caked. On her shoulder, what appeared to be a balled-up shirt was held in place by a strip of duct tape. The woman held one leg up off the ground, and she was walking on *crutches* . . . sort of. Two thick tree branches with 'y's had been crudely fashioned to fit under her arms.

He radioed for an ambulance, then ran to help her. She collapsed, unconscious, in his arms.

sixty seven

three weeks later

Anne sat alone in a snug, closet-like room. Everything about the room was small: small table, small chairs. Small ashtray. Small light fixture in the ceiling, which, at present, wasn't on. The only thing large in the room was the vast two-way mirror that she faced, looking into another room. It was bigger than the cramped quarters she sat in, with a bigger table, several more chairs, and audio recording equipment. No windows. Both rooms were as stale as gauze.

The flight from Escanaba had been long. She'd been released from the hospital after a two-week stay. Her ankle had been severely sprained, and she'd needed several dozen stitches to close up wounds she'd suffered in the dining room, including the serious puncture wound to her shoulder. The wound had become infected, prompting her to remain in the hospital an additional week. Her hand and arm had been burned. Just exactly how, she wasn't sure. She presumed the wounds came from putting out the fire that the flare had started in the bedroom. That's what the police had assumed, anyway. Anne had no recollection of the fire.

The plane ride to New York was only two hours; it was good to be home. Marta had flown Allie first to Mayo Clinic in Rochester, then, two days later, the two traveled to the Upper Peninsula. They had remained with Anne during her hospital stay, and the three had flown home together. Anne planned to fly back to upper Michigan in several weeks and retrieve her car.

At the hospital, she'd been visited by detectives, cops, more detectives. They'd even flown in someone from the FBI, from Quantico. An armed guard was placed at her door around the clock. There were a lot of questions, notes jotted down. Lots of *sorry to bother you agains* and *this'll only take a minute* and *just a few more questions, please, Ms. Harper.* But so far, she'd been the only one providing the answers, and she was getting tired of it. She had a lot of her *own* questions that she wanted answered. She was promised that they would explain as soon as *they* figured out what was going on.

Another week of rest had gone by. Anne remained home, reading manuscripts and conducting what business she could by phone. She'd been contacted two and three times a day by different law enforcement officials from all over. There had been some more questions from the FBI as well as the local suits.

And the damned tabloids. God, what a bunch of low-life bottom feeders. Offering to pay Anne if they could interview her and photograph her wounds. She hung up on them.

And finally: a call from the local precinct.

Can you come in? No more questions. Well, maybe a few. A couple. But we'll have some answers for you. One o'clock today?

The door opened beside her, and a plainclothes detective came in. He was forty-ish, balding. Dark slacks, white shirt. Tie and sport coat. Anne moved to stand, and he waved her to stay seated and spoke.

"Please." He took her outstretched hand. "I'm Detective Buren."

"Hello." She had spoken with Buren several times over the phone.

"I'm sorry that this whole thing has taken so long. As you'll find out, we're really only *beginning* to piece things together." He stressed the word *beginning* by raising his eyebrows and nodding.

Just as he finished his sentence, a door in the other room, on the other side of the two-way mirror, opened up. A uniformed policeman came in, followed by three other men.

And Gerald Morgan.

"Oh my God," Anne gasped.

"Is . . . is something wrong, Ms. Harper?"

She paused, her eyes watching Gerald Morgan as he sat down. Morgan was aware of the mirror, and had consented to her being present. Although he couldn't see her, he gave a quick glance toward the mirror, nodded, then turned his gaze to two men who sat down on the opposite side of the table. Another man sat down next to Morgan. His attorney, Anne presumed.

"Oh. No, no. Nothing," Anne finally replied to the detective.

It was Gerald Morgan . . . *sort of.*

He was clean-shaven. His scraggly beard was gone, and his hair was trimmed short. His eyes sat behind a pair gold wire-rimmed glasses. He was wearing jeans, a clean white shirt, and brown sport coat. He looked like a young college professor.

And he looked . . . *calm.* He looked at ease, confident.

Formalities were addressed, the usual. Doesn't have to answer anything if he doesn't want to, the usual legal rigamarole.

Detective Buren leaned forward and spoke quietly, his eyes focused in the opposite room.

"This thing has *exploded.* In just the last week. Hell, it's *still* blowing up." He shook his head. "It's been hell trying to keep it under wraps, away from the press. Even *they* know that something's up. We're finding out a lot more."

"How so?" Anne replied quietly. Her eyes never left Morgan.

The detective nodded toward the men in the other room. Questions had begun. Buren turned a small dial on the wall, and voices percolated through a speaker in the ceiling. Buren pointed to the speaker, directing Anne to listen.

sixty eight

"Mr. Morgan. I know you've been through all of this before. We'd like to review a few things. This is special agent Deitz—" one of the men nodded, and Gerald nodded back. "—and special agent Hayes." Gerald again dipped his head, and the detective continued. "This is *your* story, is it not?"

One of the men displayed a manuscript—*the* manuscript, the very same one Anne had read—and placed it on the table. Pages were crinkled and blood-splattered.

"Yes, it's my story. All but the last six chapters, and the pages that I specified."

"And you titled it 'Bestseller'?"

"Yes."

"When did you begin writing this story, Mr. Morgan?"

"Two years ago, thereabouts."

"Did you base 'Bestseller' on any real people, Mr. Morgan?"

"I based it on a *situation.*" His voice sounded rehearsed, like he'd answered these questions a dozen times already. Anne thought that he probably had.

"Can you explain the . . . situation?"

Morgan took a breath. "The situation was a literary agent that shunned a wanna-be writer. He stalked her at her vacation spot, intending to kill her."

"And did he? In your story?"

"No. She killed him."

The other man across from Morgan spoke. "Was this book based on an actual person, Mr. Morgan?"

The lawyer touched Morgan's arm. The two leaned together, and Gerald shook his head. The attorney folded his hand and gave a *can't say I didn't warn ya* frown.

"Yes. It was based—loosely—on Anne Harper of the Anne Harper Literary Agency."

"And why was that?"

"She . . . I knew that she vacationed at a small cottage in the Midwest. I . . . started thinking of how that would be an idea for a story. A remote location, a stalker. And the stalker would be someone she knew, someone that had a reason not to like her. Someone . . . unstable."

"Someone whom she may have refused to sign with her agency?"

"Yes."

"Your manuscripts were rejected by Ms. Harper, were they not?"

This brought a smile to Morgan's face. "Yes. All of them."

"So, *you* would have a reason—"

Morgan held up his hand. "Guys . . . we've been through this. I've told you—and you should know by now—that I had absolutely ***nothing*** to do with what's going on."

There was a few seconds of silence. Then one of the agents spoke.

"You were forcibly removed from her office, were you not?"

"Yes. It was during a time of . . . illness. A car accident, years ago, sparked a mental condition that got worse over time. Once it was discovered, I was treated with medication."

There was a long pause. Papers were reviewed, shuffled. Questions began again.

"The killer in your story. Was he based on an actual person?"

"No."

"No one in particular?"

"No one in particular at all," Morgan replied, shaking his head.

"Mark Franklin didn't make any suggestions to you about the killer or his character?"

"No."

"Not at all?"

"No. Not at all."

There was a thick silence as the two men on the far side of the table looked at some papers. The man on the left spoke.

"Have you ever been to the cabin or the lake where Ms. Harper vacations?"

"No. I went to Michigan late last summer, and stayed at a cabin at Deep Lake in the upper peninsula. I think—and this is just a guess—that it is about an hour away from where Ms. Harper vacationed. I wanted to get a feel for the land and the area while I wrote."

"Did you ever have any conversation with Ms. Harper about your book? Give her any details about what was written?"

"I haven't had any communication with Ms. Harper since my arrest a couple years ago. Until her office called a couple weeks ago, that is."

Morgan's attorney lit a cigarette, inhaled, and stretched. Exhaled. Across the table, one of the men picked up the manuscript and fingered through it.

"You wrote this on a typewriter."

"Yes."

"One copy."

"Yes. One copy."

"It was stolen?"

"Yes. By Mark Franklin."

"How do you know it was him?"

"He's the only one who knew about it. Mark and I had become . . . *acquaintances* . . . over the past few years. When he came to town for a writer's conference last year, I was telling him about the story I had just finished. Well . . . the first draft, anyway. He seemed really interested, and asked if he could look at it. I only had the one copy, but I told him if he wanted to read some of it, that would be fine. I was looking forward to his opinion. He came over and read the first draft in an afternoon."

"And he stole the final version?"

"Morgan nodded. "Three months ago. I had just finished it. I'd written a cover letter to Ms. Harper, and was going to take it to *Kinko's* to get the manuscript copied later that day after work. I wanted to get it to Anne—Ms. Harper—before she left for her vacation. She reads manuscripts while she's away, and I wanted mine to be one of them."

"But you didn't get your manuscript to her?"

"When I came home from work, the manuscript was gone. Along with my typewriter, and a bunch of other stuff. Stereo, TV. Some clothes. I reported all of that to the police." He pointed to a copy of the police report on the table.

"At the time, did you know who broke into your home?"

Morgan shook his head, closed his eyes, opened them. "No. I had no idea. I just thought it was somebody stealing things to pawn off."

"And your manuscript was missing?"

He nodded tiredly. "Yes. That's in the police report, too."

"But these last six chapters, here." The man flipped through the manuscript, pulled out a section from the bottom, and plopped it down in front of Morgan. He pulled a cigarette from a pack in his pocket, but didn't light it. Instead, he used it as a wand, pointing the unlit tip at the stack of paper on the table. "You didn't write this?"

Morgan flipped through the pages. "No."

"Not any of it?"

Morgan shook his head. "Not any of it."

"Where did you get the name 'Beth Huston'?

"From Mark," Morgan replied.

"That wasn't the original name for your character?"

"No. It was Alice Douglas. Franklin thought that particular name sounded too bland. Too out-of-date. He suggested the name Beth Huston. When I re-wrote the manuscript, I changed her name."

"And you burned your first version."

"I always do."

"Think very carefully, Mr. Morgan. Do you ever recall Mark Franklin ever talking about any stories that he was writing? Any story at all?"

Morgan thought for a moment. "No," he replied. "He spoke mostly of books that he'd read. I think I supplied you with a list of the ones Mark and I discussed."

Anne leaned toward detective Buren, a puzzled look on her face. She continued watching the conversation through the two-way, addressing detective Buren in a near whisper. *"I'm . . . I'm not getting where they're going here."*

The detective kept his eyes focused on Morgan and the men behind the mirror. He reached out, turned a dial, and the voices from the other room lowered. He spoke quietly.

"Beth Huston was the name of a woman murdered in Detroit in 1995. The things that were described in the last six chapters of the book are exactly—*to the letter*—how she was killed."

The color drained from Anne's face. Her skin crawled. *Oh my God. All of those things . . . oh Jesus. Oh God.*

"She was . . . she—" Anne couldn't find words.

Buren shook his head. "And that was just the *beginning.*"

sixty nine

In the interrogation room, stiff conversation churned. Anne watched mouths move, soundless. Detective Buren continued quietly.

"We're finding more. A woman in Indianapolis. Daytona, Miami. Even Los Angeles." Buren looked at Anne. "We've connected fifteen victims so far, all killed in the same ways."

Anne felt sick. Images of the final chapters of *Bestseller* drifted back to her, what the killer had done to Beth Huston, how he had done it. She forced them away.

"And you think—"

"We're almost positive. We've had a team over at Franklin's home almost every day. Finding more and more evidence. There's a lot we don't know. But we *do* know—" he paused, then turned to Anne. "What we *do* know is that we spoke with his former publicist at Ryerman-Golden Publishers. A Janine—"

"—Scoffield," Anne finished. "Yes." Anne and Janine Scoffield were good friends.

"Well, she confirmed that Mark Franklin was in each of those cities on the day the murders took place." He looked at her. "He was at book signings. He was out promoting *Theater of the Mine,* Ms. Harper. He was on a book tour."

Anne felt hot. Her pulse quickened, and her breathing was rapid. It was an off balance feeling, like her brain had been leaning back in a chair and had gone too far and had to catch itself before tumbling backward.

"You okay?" Buren asked.

"Yeah, yeah. Fine."

"Like I said . . . we're still putting it together. But as close as we can tell, he was leading a double-life *big time.* He was married with three daughters; you know all that. He fooled everyone, including his wife, about his first book. Or, rather, Caroline Yates's book. Well, Mark Franklin was a writer, all right. He wrote *everything* down. In 1993, he began to write a book about a serial killer. His research led him to interview dozens of killers behind bars. We've already talked to several that remember him. He asked them what it felt like to watch someone die, to see the last light in their eyes, to hear their last breath."

Anne cringed. More visions from *Bestseller* swam in her head, and again she shoved them off.

"The cons we interviewed all told us the same thing," Buren continued. "They said Mark Franklin didn't want to *write* about a serial killer. He wanted to *become one.* His 'research' took him to sadomasochistic porn shops, S&M bars, bondage boutiques, shit like that. He became obsessed with pain. Gave him power. And yet, everyone we've talked with says the same thing: nice guy, give you the shirt off his back. Close neighbors and friends, anyway. You knew him fairly well yourself."

"I thought I did."

"So did a lot of other people. There was a part of this guy that was Richie Cunningham. There was another part of him that was so far gone he was on his way back around."

"So why Caroline? Why her?" Anne asked.

Detective Buren shrugged. "Who knows? Easy target, perhaps. For such a high-profile woman, she was pretty accessible. Maybe he knew her. That's not real clear yet. She wasn't killed in the same fashion that he'd murdered his other victims. She was murdered early on, before—"

He stopped and switched gears. "We *do* believe that Ms. Yates was his first victim. That event was probably what gave him an initial taste of . . . power. Or whatever he felt." Then: "I'm sure we'll have some more answers soon. Franklin kept a very . . . *descriptive* book. The last six chapters that he'd written, the ones you read, were copied verbatim, as far as we can tell, from his book he'd been writing. No one ever caught up with him because he was able to bounce around the country so much. With three daughters, his wife couldn't join him. It's bizarre, I know. But it's piecing together. And the puzzle is pretty damned ugly."

Anne heaved a long, slow breath. "I just can't believe—"

Buren touched her arm and nodded toward the men in the other room. "Here. I wanted you to hear this." He turned the dial and the voices from the speaker grew louder. One of the men was flipping through the manuscript. He handed it to Morgan.

"So, you have no idea what happened to the last six chapters of your book?"

"Eight. There are eight missing, along with a number of pages throughout the manuscript. No, I don't know where they went."

"You don't think that somehow, maybe, they might have found their way to the Anne Harper Literary Agency?"

Morgan shook his head. "No. No I don't. It would have been impossible."

"You burned your first draft. Personally."

"Yes. In a barrel in back of my apartment building."

"In your original version—yours, now, not these six chapters here—the woman, Beth Huston, kills the stalker?"

"Yes."

"And how does she kill him?"

The two men across from Morgan turned, looking directly into the two way mirror. They couldn't see her, but they knew that she was there.

Morgan turned, looked directly into the mirror, and spoke. Detective Buren turned, waiting to see Anne's expression.

"A wine bottle opener," Morgan replied. *In my story, she killed the man with a compressed air wine bottle opener."*

seventy

Anne met Gerald Morgan in the hall, but only briefly. Nothing was said beyond strained greetings, then Morgan continued past Anne, followed by his attorney. Buren remained at Anne's side.

"Down here."

Detective Buren led her to a door at the end of a bright hall. He tapped a numerical code into a keypad on the wall. There was a low buzzing sound, and a click. Buren grasped the handle and walked into the room. Several people worked, sitting and standing. None turned to acknowledge the visitors.

"Over here."

Buren led her to a long table, stacked with papers, items sealed in plastic bags, pens, and pencils. Buren turned.

"Rick?" he called out. A moment later a man arrived carrying a clear plastic bag. He handed it to Buren, who looked at it, then handed the bag to Anne. Inside were a pair of bundled panties. Off white, high-cut.

"Size small, *Victoria's Secret,*" Buren explained. "Look familiar?"

Anne flipped the bag over in her hand. "As in *mine?*" She flipped the bag over again. "I guess it's possible." Anne had several that were identical to the pair in the bag. She handed the bag back to the detective.

"These were found in Franklin's pocket," he explained. He had—"

"—written about it in the story," Anne finished, her voice flat and dazed. Buren nodded. "There were several pages throughout the book that Franklin had re-written to mimic the things he had done to Beth Huston."

And that's why some of the parts in the book didn't make sense, Anne thought. *It was Franklin writing . . . not Morgan.*

"The wine opener," Anne said, staring at Detective Buren. She tried to read his thoughts before he spoke, tried to unmask twenty-five years of cop all in one glare, but it was impossible. "Why had Franklin left the wine opener right out in the open? I mean . . . if the character in Morgan's book had used it to kill the stalker, why would Franklin—"

She was interrupted by Buren's shaking head. "That's why we couldn't figure this thing out," he replied. "Franklin is—*was*—obviously highly intelligent. Early on, we had no idea who had done what, or for what reason. That's why security was so tight while you were in the hospital. But the wine opener . . . who knows? That may have been Franklin's way of pumping his ego even more. To know that you had the power to kill him, right there, but he wasn't going to let you do it. Or, in his *mind* he wasn't going to let you do it. Hell, Anne, I don't know. Figure out Franklin's motive and it'd be worth a Pulitzer."

Buren handed the bag back to the man who had brought it, and the man strode off. He gestured for Anne to have a seat behind a finger-smudged computer monitor. Anne sat down; Buren wheeled a chair over from another table and seated himself next to her. His attention was on the screen, and he tapped at a beige keypad below the monitor.

The screen blinked, then displayed a map of the United States. "Here," he began, tapping the keys again. New York City blinked red. A date flashed next to it.

"March 12th, 1991," Buren said, reading the date on the screen. His eyes glowed, reflecting the images on the monitor. "The date of Caroline Yates's murder." He tapped the keys again, and over a dozen cities began to blink red, each one accompanied by a different date. Then, a single line began in New York City, criss-crossing the United States as it connected with the various blinking cities. The image on the monitor looked like a child's connect-the-dots with no purpose. No funny clown or cartoon character or smiling horse.

Then: more tapping on the keypad. Below each date in each city, a name appeared.

A woman's name.

"This is what we believe to be Franklin's pattern that started here—" he pointed to Detroit on the screen —"beginning with Beth Huston, May 25th, 1995. From Detroit, he went here, to Las Vegas. Yvonne Stead, May 30th. She was twenty-five."

"What about Caroline Yates?"

"That was earlier. It's—*she's*—not charted because her murder was a few years before he really got on a roll."

Anne watched, bewildered, as Buren followed the line across the country, showing the killer's path. Then he tapped the keys again, and still another name appeared beneath each city. Anne read one of the names aloud, puzzled.

"Borders Books & Music?"

Buren nodded. "This was Mark Franklin's book signing schedule," he said.

"This is unbelievable," Anne whispered. "It's—"

"Best we can tell, the murders began around a time when things weren't going so well. He couldn't get any more book deals, sales of his first book weren't going to keep him going financially. His wife said he became infuriated with the publishing industry, and increasingly maddened by the day-to-day pressures of surviving. They separated, finally divorced. She said that he went off the deep end, got into some cocaine problems."

Anne nodded slightly. She'd heard that he had been into drugs for a time, but she wasn't sure to what extent.

"In 1994," Buren continued, "three years after the murder of Yates, he told his ex-wife that he finally had an idea for a book. Worked on it night and day. His ex says she knows this because he frequently canceled his weekend visitations with his three daughters to write. Once, when he hadn't arrived to pick them up, she drove to his house. Found him at his computer, writing. Said he smelled like he hadn't showered in days. House was a mess. Franklin went off, slapped her around, told her never to come over again."

"This is when he started visiting the killers? In prison?" Anne asked.

Buren nodded. "Around that time, yes," he said. "What we believe Mark Franklin did was to write a book that simply *couldn't* be ignored. He began writing it in 1994, and now the book is—*was*—almost finished."

Buren stood up and stepped over to a shelf. He picked up an enormous hand-bound book. It was shoddily put together, and the pages seemed well-worn. The cover was black leather; it, too, was quite worn, like a scuffed cowhide jacket.

"This was found in Franklin's house. The book is about the exploits of a serial killer. No . . . *worse.* The character wasn't *just* a serial killer. The main character was deranged in ways that are unimaginable. The story follows the killer as he selects his victims, details what the killer did to them, how they were disposed of. Pages and pages about how the torturing made him feel, how the victims reacted to him. How he was certain that, when finished, his book would be a worldwide sensation, of sorts."

Anne reached to open the cover of the book. Detective Buren placed a protective hand on it, and Anne stopped, withdrew.

"In 1995, Mark Franklin began his spree. According to his publicist, this would have been about the time that his popularity had really faded from view. He hadn't had any new books, and it had been difficult to schedule a book tour without a new work to promote. But they had managed to put together a meager 'tour' of sorts. It was then that he began living his other 'book', so to speak. He chose victims based on the characters he'd written about in his manuscript. After each murder, he'd go back into his computer and change the name of the fictional victim, replacing it with the name of the *real* victim. He'd also change details, such as what color hair she had, physical features . . . stuff like that. Then he'd add in digital photographs of—"

Anne closed her eyes.

"Ms. Harper?"

She opened her eyes, nodded.

"This isn't anything we need to go over, unless—"

"Yes, please." Anne wasn't searching for answers, as much as she was searching for—

"Several weeks ago," Buren continued, "Franklin was nearing completion. He had only one more victim to complete the book. He had chosen his victim, and left spaces in the pages for pictures." Buren breathed deeply, exhaled. He raised his eyebrows and looked at Anne. "The last victim was *you*, Ms. Harper. You were supposed to be the end of the book."

Heat burned from temple to temple. It was more than just bizarre. It was madness. Pure, psychotic madness. Anne's flesh felt grimy and dirty. Her face felt as if it were sliding from her skull.

"What's most unusual," Buren added, reaching for the huge book, "is this." He opened the cover. "Franklin started this in 1994. We know this from his computer registry. In 1994, this is what he titled the book. Before he even *met* Gerald Morgan." He turned the book towards Anne, allowing her to read the title page.

Bestseller. In 1994, before Mark Franklin began the murders, while he was still plotting, he had called his book *Bestseller.*

She put her face in her hands. Tears had formed, and she wiped them away. She was trembling. She spoke, her breath only a whisper.

"There was no reason," she said. She shook her head. "No reason . . . ."

"There never is," Buren said quietly. Paused. Then: "We know the *whats,* the *whens.* We know the *hows* and *wheres.* We just don't know the *whys.* I don't think we ever will. We don't know where they come from. How they think, what they think." He sighed. It was a tired sigh, a sigh of complete exasperation. He hunched his shoulders in a bewildered shrug. "Sometimes the monsters just show up, Anne. Sometimes they are just . . . *here.* All we can do is try to stop them."

The afternoon was gray and cold. Rain fell. The air was clammy and smelled of September. A haze had settled over New York, a swirling, moist phantom that haunted skyscrapers, alleys, parks and streets.

A yellow cab pulled into a cemetery, winding slowly beneath the still, dark trees. Finally, the vehicle stopped. Anne emerged, telling the driver to wait. He answered in Spanish, nodding his head.

Anne walked through the cluttered stones, grayed and aged, wet with rain. Her shoes were soon soaked, she didn't notice.

She stopped at Caroline Yates's grave and stood for a long time. Thoughts and feelings rushed into her mind. Images, emotions, flashes of the past. She tried to stop them, tried to push them off. They were visions of Caroline Yates, all smiling and happy, trying to catch Anne's bouquet at the wedding reception. Of Gerald Morgan wild-eyed in her office, smashing the coffee table. Of Mark Franklin, God, no, Mark Franklin. The cabin, the hummingbirds. Feelings of terror and bewilderment. Everything came rushing to her at once, speeding by in fast-forward. Rewind, then fast-forward. Candace. Cliff Stevenson. Dr. Gardner. And—

Allie. Images of a frail child, her body wasted and gaunt in a hospital bed, beaten to near death by an unseen beast inside of her. Holding Allie in her arms all night when she'd been told that she wasn't going to make it, trying to savor every moment, every precious second.

Sometimes the monster comes out of nowhere, Anne, she remembered Dr. Gardner telling her. *There are no reasons. He just shows up. There's nothing you could have done differently.*

Anne knelt in the wet grass, and wept.